ANONASAI

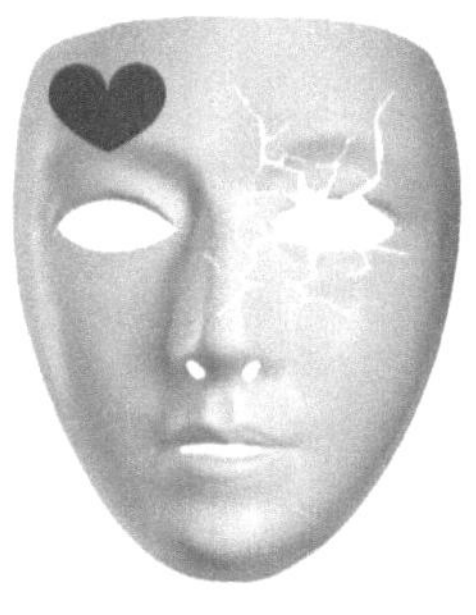

JASMINE HIND

Published in Australia by Sid Harta Books & Print Pty Ltd,

ABN: 34632585293

23 Stirling Crescent, Glen Waverley, Victoria 3150 Australia

Telephone: +61 3 9560 9920, Facsimile: +61 3 9545 1742

E-mail: author@sidharta.com.au

First published in Australia 2023

This edition published 2023

Copyright © Jasmine Hind 2023

Cover design, typesetting: WorkingType (www.workingtype.com.au)

Jasmine Hind

Anonasai

ISBN: 978-1-922958-25-9

ABOUT THE AUTHOR

Jasmine Hind was born and raised on the Sunshine Coast, Queensland. She is an educator in Early Childhood and Education with hobbies including reading, writing, painting and many more creative things. When she is not busy creating, Jasmine enjoys the company of her family and friends. On Alexandra Headland and Mooloolaba beaches, she loves to listen to the sound of the waves, smell the salty air, and enjoy the relaxing environment. Her biggest weakness is book stores, as she always says she's just going to have a look and ends up coming out with an armful of books.

ACKNOWLEDGEMENTS

I would like to thank my family — Amanda Bullock, Kathleen Batson, Maree Hind, Tony Hind and Steven Morrow — for all their help and constructive support when my novel was still in the early stages. Thank you to the team at Sid Harta Publishers for making my dream of becoming an author a reality — a big thank you to Kerry B. Collison for recognising my potential. To Marie Pietersz and Luke Harris: I could not have published my work without your expertise. To my editor, Denise M Taylor: thank you for your time, editing skill and feedback.

CHAPTER 1

L iving in a villa off the grid is a woman of unknown age. Every morning she walked around her property inspecting her camera system to ensure security. Her fiery red hair glowed in the morning sunlight, contrasting beautifully with her black clothing. She smiled at her mobile phone as she appeared on her camera system.

Walking to her last camera, a notification popped up on her screen. *Motion detected in the north entrance.* She tapped on the alert, her emerald-green eyes narrowing as she analysed the live feed to see a figure in black clothing with a white mask.

As she walked to the north entrance, she cut through her marble kitchen. The red-haired woman grabbed her white mask made of a secret material. She had black fractures on her left eye, and on the opposite side of her face there was a painted purple heart above the eye that stretched down the face and stopped beside the mask's white lips. The feature she loved most was the purple heart.

She approached the figure with caution and then suddenly stopped.

'What do you want, brother?'

The man bowed respectfully, then said, 'I'm not him. The Head sent me here to give you this, ma'am.' The man held out a white envelope.

Annoyingly, a distorting device obscured his normal voice; even more annoying, her brother sent a subordinate. She hadn't seen her brother since her banishment from the Makino clan, but that was a long time ago.

She hesitantly looked at the envelope for a while. She hated envelopes; *how many people have handled it?* Then she saw the subordinate wearing gloves. So, she took the envelope then walked away, back into her kitchen. Grabbing a knife and opening the letter she saw a demand. She couldn't deny it as it was official. She'd ignored the others as they were boring and lacked excitement, but she thought this one could be fun.

The demand was to assassinate a figurehead.

Most of the information was in code, but she knew where to go by the photo. She went into her bathroom and took out some black hair dye.

She dyed her red hair raven black then grabbed a red

sports bag from her wardrobe with gear and equipment inside. She threw in some clothes and essentials she would need for the next several weeks and did one final sweep of her property before locking her house with a single tap on her phone.

The woman in all black got into her vintage 2020 black Honda NSX replica and headed to the airport. The traffic was perfect, just missing peak hour. She was halfway there when she noticed she had a tail. To ensure she wasn't being paranoid, she changed lanes. Unfortunately, the silver charger also changed lanes. *Was it a coincidence?* She changed lanes once more and watched as the charger in her rear-view mirror changed lanes again. It was confirmed: they were following her. She redirected her concentration back to the front of her car with only seconds to spare, as she was rapidly approaching the back-end of an old-fashioned delivery truck. Her tyres screeched as she slammed on the brakes. She stopped mere centimetres from the truck's rear door that had had suddenly swung open. The vehicles behind her swerved, narrowly avoiding a collision. They beeped their horns, and hurled abuse. She didn't care. She looked in her rear-view mirror to see the charger behind her. The windows were blacked-out and the windscreen blackened, identifying the driver or passengers impossible. She wondered about their driving and tracking skills.

As the truck pulled away, now was the time to find out.

She smirked before putting her foot down; smoke filled the back wheel compartment as she took off, the charger sped after her. Both cars snaked through traffic as if the other cars didn't exist. The pursuer was proficient and persistent; no matter how hard she tried to shake them, the silver charger caught up with the Honda. The driver in the silver charger got gutsy and moved in for a pit manoeuvre. As it moved closer, she increased her speed and the Honda went under a hovering flat tray, then down an off-ramp.

She smiled as she slowed her speed and saw the charger speed past realising that they had failed to see where she went. So, she drove into a carpark before finding a parking spot. It wasn't long before they came back.

She heard the charger coming up the concrete multi-level carpark's ramp, so she drove three spaces forward as her car's colour changed from black to royal blue. She opened her Honda app and pressed the LED licence plate on her phone, instantly changing her plate from 839 BFT to GOTU11. The charger passed her to the next level. She smiled once more before exiting her vehicle.

She walked to the airport entrance, only to notice it was different. The South Row Airport was new, with tiled flooring instead of carpet and coloured laser lines were used as indicators for each gate. There were scanners for implanted chips for those who were in a hurry, but she preferred the old-fashioned method. She entered a first-class lounge with a golden archway with security. The archway was an eyesore as she knew it was a shabby imitation. Then there was the less-technical side with semi-circular marble desks with attendants in purple and gold uniforms behind them.

She groaned at the staff's uniform colour choice. These were colours of the royals, not for ordinary people to wear. *At least staff at Park Airport wore khaki-coloured shirts with black pants in 1909.* She walked up to the marble desk of a Transport Security Administration officer to check in with her phone. The woman had blonde hair tied back and wore limited make-up. The TSA woman looked at the photo on her screen then at her current customer.

'Any reason to go to...'

'That is my reason, not yours.'

The TSA woman pointed to a sign above her head. Her eyes looked up to that sign that read 'Rudeness Will NOT BE tolerated'.

She sighed. 'Fine, a family matter I need to deal with.'

The TSA woman analysed her passport. 'You understand, Miss Kaisøn, that you will be heading into a one-way zone.'

'Yes, I'm aware there will be no help if I get into misfortune.'

The TSA woman looked at Miss Kaisøn then nodded, signalling approval. She wasn't appropriately dressed for the cold climate or a war zone for that matter. The blacked-haired woman walked away before the TSA woman could ask any more questions. She looked at her digital ticket on her phone and saw the colour outline, then followed the pink laser line to Gate 7.

She slid her fake passport into her red sports bag then patiently waited for the plane. She had four hours to plan for mishaps. *That silver charger wouldn't leave me alone. Perhaps they have lost me for good.* She closed her eyes and listened to people talking. Sound eased in then out as she was close to sleep. She started to smell burning flesh and a male voice called her name frantically before flames flickered before her eyes.

CHAPTER 2

She was close to sleep when flashbacks disturbed her, then something cold was pressed against her neck. She didn't move as she could tell it was the muzzle of a gun.

'Everyone out, don't move!' ordered a man.

'You don't want an audience?' she replied toyingly.

Her emerald-green eyes darted around the transit lounge, taking in their expressions of shock, worry and fear. She then caught their reflection in a viewing mirror in the top left-hand corner of the room to see the male in dark colours. She saw his gun; a standard 9-millimetre Glock still on its safety and a man's shadow. A smile slowly stretched across her face as she stood.

'I said *don't* move,' yelled the man.

'And when did you say that?' she asked with a thick English accent.

'When he pointed the gun at your head,' replied an Asian officer.

She looked at the undercover officer as he rose; she showed no recognition as he stood to her left. He was older; his hair had started to recede. As he stood there, she could see a few grey hairs glistening in the LED lights. She thought, *There are a few wrinkles lining his face now, but at least his fashion sense hadn't wavered.* The last time she saw him was in Tokyo, and she could still recognise his voice.

'There is no need for conflict, Officer Cunnings,' Officer Hyosuke warned. 'She will come easily, so holster your weapon.'

'You make it sound like you know her,' hissed Officer Cunnings.

'I've had run-ins with her before, yes.'

She looked over her right shoulder to see an open door before returning her attention to Hyosuke.

'You're not faster than a bullet,' warned Cunnings.

She called his bluff and ran for the door; Cunnings fired his gun only to hear a click. The officer looked at his gun in confusion before she took out a tranquiliser from under her jumper and fired. The American officer fell to the ground with a silver dart in his right thigh.

Hyosuke walked forward to find the dart sticking out of the American before looking at his friend.

'When did you start carrying a gun?' asked Hyosuke.

'Right after I left the Makino. They don't have control over me.'

She returned her tranquiliser under her jumper before walking to the sleeping officer and removing the dart. Hyosuke stood behind her now.

'You knew he'd shoot.'

'His gun was on safety.'

Hyosuke looked at the fallen gun to see it was, in fact, on safety.

'Where are you going, Anonasai?'

'On a mission. Somewhere cold.'

'A lot of countries are in winter this time of year.'

A man's voice came over the airport system. *'Gate five is now open. Plane JB 706 is now boarding for Tokyo, Japan.'*

Officer Hyosuke grabbed his luggage and walked towards the door.

'Hyosuke, you didn't go for your weapon. Are you off duty?'

'Yes, I am going back home. Also, you shot the American who was seeing me off.'

'He should've known better about carrying a gun in this place.'

Hyosuke smiled and Anonasai returned the gesture. 'I had to return the favour for Osaka. I hate owing favours. Now we're even.'

'I know ... see you around, Hunting Bird.'

'See you around, Hyosuke.'

As Officer Hyosuke leaves, Officer Cunnings groaned as he gained consciousness. He held his neck and blinked the fogginess away to see medics treating him.

'Where... where is that woman...?'

'What woman?' asked a supervisor on site.

The room was empty apart from two medics and three officers, Cunnings' friends on the force and his boss.

'That woman from the most-wanted list was here. Ann ... Anon ...'

'Anonasai!? The wandering killer?' snapped a dark-skinned officer.

Cunnings looked at his colleague and read the dark-skinned officer's name, Iggy.

'Yeah, that's the one.'

'Dude, you didn't call for backup. You have balls,' said an officer with a Texan accent.

Officer Cunnings looked over to his right and saw the brown-haired officer. He looked at the name badge and read it twice to see Officer James Whippet's name.

'Enough ... you are lucky you're not dead. Anonasai is known to kill without mercy. She is wanted in one hundred and ninety-five countries,' stated Sergeant Hitchcock.

Cunnings looked at his boss. His short, copper-red hair looked strawberry-blonde under the LED lights. He wore all black with three stripes on his shoulders to indicate his sergeant rank. His name was displayed on a golden badge

— Sergeant Michael Hitchcock. 'Why, she doesn't look that deadly to …'

'Man, have you read her file?' questioned a medic.

'No, only the wanted poster.'

'Give him some slack. He is still a rookie,' said Officer Iggy.

'Hey, CJ, what happened to the cop you were protecting?' asked Officer Whippet.

He looked confused as no one answered this question. He noticed everyone staring at him expectantly. Then it hit him. He was CJ.

Upon this sudden revelation, CJ pulled out his phone to see the tracker he had planted, wondering if Officer Hyosuke was heading towards Japan or New Zealand. CJ looked at the tiny blue dot on the screen before tapping on the bubble to see if it was travelling to its destination.

'Kotoshi Hyosuke knew Anonasai. He said she would come easily if I put my gun away.'

All three officers looked at each other and then at CJ, trying to find answers among themselves. They left the airport, none of them coming to anything but speculatory conclusions. CJ would have to sleep off the side-effects and make his report when he was back at the precinct.

Officer Whippet thought over what his friend said, but it didn't make sense. *Why would someone in witness protection know one of the most wanted people in the world?* Perhaps it was the ketamine talking, but his gut told him otherwise, so he'd follow it up with the FBI division. *My friends in the CIA could help, or perhaps that girl who owes me one in Interpol. Anyway, even if Iggy, CJ and their supervisor Hitchcock didn't know, Officer Whippet always got the answers.*

Officer Iggy assisted CJ into his cruiser before driving off. Whippet climbed into his cruiser and waited for Supervisor Hitchcock to leave before making a phone call.

Whippet hears five rings on the line before a female answered.

'Lana.'

'Whippet of the USA or my Whippet?'

'Both.'

'Are you on duty?'

'Yes.'

'Then you're Whippet of the USA.'

'Okay fine.'

A beep ensured the call was secured. 'Go ahead.'

'Listen, I need that favour we talked about.'

'Which one? The one between us or the dirty one?'

'I haven't forgotten about that, but that is beside the point ... I mean the favour about the Japanese officer.'

'Oh, that one. Are you still digging into that guy? With Officer Hyosuke in your care, I thought you would have everything, or do you need something else?'

'I need to know if he had contact with a most wanted person — a woman.'

'I'll do my best, but it will cost you.'

'Let me know later.'

Officer Whippet ended the call then drove away before getting a call back.

'That was fast, Lana.'

'That's a nice name, but sadly I'm not Lana,' replied a distorted voice.

Whippet pulled over and started to trace the phone call. 'Okay, I'll bite. Who is this?'

'Your fellow officers went after an outcast of mine. Her name will ring a bell for Officer CJ Cunnings.'

'The head of Makino clan, I assume?'

The man on the line chuckled, but on the phone, it made the sound more auto-tuned with a warped effect. 'Sharp as ever, Officer.'

'How did you get this number? This is a restricted line for police officers only.'

'There are no such restrictions for the Makino clan. We have many ways to get answers, as do you. You will call off the bounty hunters chasing Anonasai, and the American police department in South Row will not interfere with her work.'

'I can't guarantee that, and I don't know anything about bounty hunters.'

'The silver charger belongs to a Rem Hitchcock from your police department.' He sighed. 'It's a shame ... I could use a hacker who covers her tracks like that.' He laughed menacingly.

What an asshole, Whippet thought. *Thirty more seconds and I'd have his location.*

Whippet continued toying with the man. 'Don't you have hackers? Like one codenamed Ping, Court and Truth?'

A distorted growl is heard on the other side of the line. 'I see you have done some digging into my clan. No matter.'

'We're close to cracking the Red Feather case, since outcasts are no trouble for you … they will be in our custody.'

'You have your instructions. Fail, and you know the rest.'

The line went dead as the tracking system landed on a mansion in the hills. Officer Whippet sped towards police headquarters.

Whippet stormed through the glass doors and up the stairs to Sergeant Hitchcock's office, who was already in a meeting with Officer Iggy.

'Sorry to interrupt, sir, but I believe that the Makino clan's base of operation is in the Oak Mountains.'

Sergeant Hitchcock's face reddens as his blood pressure rises. Iggy shakes his head, as this is the third time Whippet has said this.

'You interrupt my meeting with Iggy because you believe you found a make-believe clan's base?!'

'The Makino clan is not make-believe, sir. The Head called me on the way back from the airport, and I traced that call to this mansion in the Oak Mountains, sir.'

Sergeant Hitchcock grabbed Whippet's printout, crumpling it up. 'Get out!'

Whippet left before something heavier than paper was thrown at him.

'Sir, Whippet is the only one assigned on the Makino case,' commented Officer Iggy.

'I know, Iggy, the others went mad. I hate to see a fine officer like him to go that way.'

'Perhaps we should hear him out, sir. He seems pretty sure this time.'

Sergeant Hitchcock watched Whippet through a glass door as he stormed down a white hallway and into a break room. They believed the Makino clan was fake. No one believed his findings, *but I can prove their authenticity with evidence of the clan's existence. It was no lie that the taskforce had many members, and within weeks they all drove themselves crazy. No, it wasn't that simple; I've reviewed their notes to the letter, and I haven't gone mad. Someone had gotten to them.*

Whippet was safe within the building's four walls. He held his head in his hands as theories and conspiracies flooded his mind.

Could the Makino clan make a person go mad? Do they even have the power or the personnel? What if I missed something that could do this? It would have to be someone very skilled. No, they can't, or can they? But poison can; they can track people ... listen to yourself, James ... You sound like a fucking mad man. Anyone can follow anyone.

'Officer Whippet!'

James turned to the door to see a junior officer standing there — a female with black hair and blue eyes.

'Yeah, yes?'

'A person in holding wants to make a statement. So, Sergeant Hitchcock sent me to get you.'

'Can't the sergeant take it?'

'Yes, sir, but it's about some Red Feather case. A case you are handling.'

James walked to the holding cells to see a blonde female wearing all black sitting in an eight-by-eight-foot cell with four padded benches. Whippet walked in front of the blonde and looked into her chocolate-brown eyes.

'What's your name, miss?'

'You have my file.'

A loud bang echoed through the silence behind the lady as Sergeant Hitchcock slammed a baton on the iron bars. The blonde lady jumped then turned to see the sergeant behind her, a yellow file in his left hand.

'My officer asked you for your name, madam. Do remember your manners.'

She groaned before answering, 'Liz Flames. In the Makino I went by the name Oxy.'

Sergeant Hitchcock opened the yellow file to corroborate

her information. Whippet's ears picked up on Makino.

'What do you mean *went by*?'

'I used to be in that clan. Then I was banished like the other members.'

'Other members? How many outcasts are there?'

'Myself and Anonasai that I know of. We don't stay connected, once an outcast. The clan is forbidden to reach out. You start a new life, so to speak.'

'What was your job in the Makino clan?' questioned Officer Whippet.

Liz hesitated before answering, 'I was the Skeuopoios.'

'Excuse me?' asked Sergeant Hitchcock.

'I was the Skeuopoios.'

'I heard, but what is that?'

'Mask maker,' answered Liz with little interest.

'Why not just say that?' hissed Sergeant Hitchcock, getting irritated.

'Skeuopoios is the proper title. However, Anonasai said that people of this era make a fuss.'

'What did you say?' asked James.

'Skeuopoios is the proper title....' repeated Liz.

'About Anonasai ...' interrupted James.

'She said people of this era do make a fuss.'

Sergeant Hitchcock looked at Whippet as he grabbed the iron bars, making his knuckles white.

'*Era* ... why would Anonasai say that? Why not the

fifty-first century.'

'Because she isn't...' Liz stopped herself and looked at Whippet, then the sergeant, as the arrogant man circled the cell.

'Liz, please. I only want to help you,' pleaded James. 'Tell me what you know of the wandering assassin, and we can protect you from the Makino clan. We can make the assault charges disappear.'

Liz looked at Officer Whippet with a disapproving glare, then laughed.

'Protect me from them? Anonasai is my best ally from the clan, and that officer got what he deserved. Groping a woman like that.'

'James, Oxy made masks for the whole clan. White, plain, and I have to say perfect. No string needed to hold them in place. However, I see a flaw.'

'Excuse me!' hissed Liz

'You used a plaster-base medium to hold your masks in place, but they quickly broke. So, then you used a secret medium that fixed that issue. However, when we examined your mask, it had a few shimmering areas, and it crumbled like dust when I shot a certain spot.'

'You, you destroyed my mask!' yelled Liz jumping to her feet.

'Yeah, but you can make a new one ... right? You are a mask maker.'

'How dare you! I don't break....'

'But you did. You broke two of the officer's ribs when you punched him,' stated Sergeant Hitchcock.

Liz looked at the sergeant with daggers. James loosened his grip on the iron bars. Sergeant Hitchcock paused his walk around the cell and continued his interrogation.

'You have an outstanding warrant in Scotland. I wonder what that is for?'

Liz looked at the ground and crossed her arms.

Sergeant Hitchcock slammed the file closed and exited the room.

'Liz, what's the warrant for?' questioned Officer Whippet.

'Assault. I defended myself against my father, who was a violent drunk. By the time the police officers arrived, he'd sobered up and lied. He told them I was the violent one,' she said with venom. 'I was going to the police station when my entire world went sideways. The van got hit and rolled a few times. The officers were drugged. That's when I met her.'

'Who? Met who?' James was starting to sound desperate.

'Anonasai. She got me out of the wreckage and gave me a choice – join her clan of the Makino or go to jail for a crime I didn't commit. So, I joined her clan.'

'Her clan? But The Head owns the clan.'

'Anonasai has her own followers – she handpicked them. It's a splinter group. There are Ping, Sax, a few others and me.'

'Earlier, you said *era*. What did you mean?'

'That wasn't for you to hear.'

'Please, my offer still stands — no wait, I'll better the deal. I'll drop all charges and wipe your file.'

'That's against the law, even for you, Officer.' Liz looked at James. He didn't move. She looked at his eyes to see he did not waver; he was waiting for her to make her judgment. The window of this opportunity would close soon, so Liz walked up to the iron bars in front of Whippet. 'If you must know …'

He leaned in closer as she whispered her answer. 'She comes from 1666.'

His eyes widened in shock. James pushed himself from the bars and looked at Liz. *She wasn't lying. No, she spoke the truth. But how?*

He walked to the exit and Liz yelled after him, 'Officer Whippet! You promised!'

James turned to face Liz. 'I know. I'll free you.' He then walked out and straight to his computer.

Liz curled herself into a ball and muttered, 'I'm sorry, Anonasai.' Then she silently stared at the floor.

CHAPTER 3

After a twelve-hour flight, Anonasai checked her luggage out and headed to a hotel. She noticed that this war-torn country was nothing like the Republic of Telfax. This country had barely any damage. The people walked around without fear. She walked down a narrow asphalt street lined with brick buildings of various sizes and colours. As Anonasai walked through the town she heard snippets of the locals' conversation in their native tongue.

Anonasai walked past a few people and noticed that they have fallen silent. *Have they become aware of me?* She looked at a few citizens to see no one was looking at her, but behind her. Suddenly, a small object torpedoed through the sky like lightning. Subsequently, a roar echoed in the troposphere before an eerie siren rang out. At first everything was still. Anonasai watched as all the colour drained from the people's faces. Chaos erupted as parents grabbed their fear-stricken children as they cried and refused to move. Some were abandoned as people collided with each other. Limbs were red and badly twisted, even some bones were broken bones in the process as shelters filled.

Mass panic soon took over for the crowd to find any sort of cover. There were screams as people shouted names, but through all the chaos, Anonasai glided through the panic like a ghost until a warm hand grabbed her arm.

'Come, come!' urged a woman tugging on her arm.

Anonasai looked in the direction where the late-forty-something woman was trying to take her. Anonasai shouted at her, 'No! You stay there, and you will die. That structure isn't safe.'

The woman looked at the shelter and saw nothing wrong, but now there was hesitation. The woman abandoned her attempt to save the stranger on the street and got her children to another shelter.

Unfortunately, an explosion occurred three and a half kilometres away. Anonasai felt the impact through her feet before hiding in an ally and she covered her ears as the shock wave hit. Dust filled the street, followed by rumbling thunder.

Minutes passed as shocked locals moved from shelters and crawled out of spaces to assess the damage. Glass shards littered the ground and three buildings had collapsed polluting the air with dust and fine building material. A group of people stood around one collapsed building as a crawl space was no longer. Citizens started to dig through the rumble. A woman stopped them by yelling at them in Escaian that she was okay and no one was there. An argument soon broke out as the other people insisted on searching through the rubble.

Anonasai stood far away as the woman held her two children close.

'How did you know that building wasn't safe?' questioned a tan-skinned Englishman in dusty clothing.

Anonasai looked the man up and down as he dusted himself off and walked away.

He called after her, 'Hey, you know it's considered rude to walk away when someone is talking to you.'

Anonasai rounded a corner and waited for the eager Englishman to follow. She hid her red sports bag in a wooden crate and turned it around to the wall before hiding herself. The Englishman rounded the corner, saw a dark alley and swore when he was pinned to the cold brick wall with a knife to his throat.

'Easy … on my belt you'll see a badge.'

'I saw. What do you want?'

'Nothing, love. I'm looking for a figurehead with a target on his head.'

Are we after the same target? This would be problematic, thought Anonasai.

Anonasai raised an eyebrow as the Englishman kneed her in the stomach. She punched the bricks near his head and they crumbled. The Englishman dodged before drawing his firearm. Anonasai stood side on with her knife in hand. The man observed her right hand to see no bruising, no blood, only debris on her knuckles as she stood, staring him down.

'What happened to your eyes? They were green before, now they're white.'

Anonasai blinked twice as her irises returned emerald green.

'You're Hunting Bird? Anonasai Hunting Bird.'

Anonasai narrowed her brow before angling her knife.

'I'm allied with Officer Kotoshi Hyosuke,' disclosed the Englishman.

'How do you know Hyosuke?'

Anonasai slowly lowered her knife and the Englishman lowered his gun as locals walked past.

'I met him in Osaka. My men and I were under fire, and that silver fox saved us. So, I still owe that man a favour.'

As locals passed them, then disappeared out of view, the Englishman pointed his gun again, but Anonasai held her knife beside her.

'You know my name. I am yet to know yours.'

'Detective Noah Bondi.'

Anonasai sleeved her knife before grabbing her sports bag from the wooden crate and leaving the alley. Detective Bondi stood in the alley, confused for a moment before catching up with her. Anonasai sighed as she hoped he wasn't going to pursue her.

'All right, Detective, are you protecting this figurehead?'

'That's classified. I should report that you are …'

'You won't and can't.' Anonasai holds up a black phone above her right shoulder before pocketing it.

Detective Bondi patted his pockets before catching up to her once more.

'That's police property. How did you get that!'

'I have swift hands.'

'Can I have it back?'

'No'

'And why not?'

'I have my reasons.'

Anonasai turned into a hotel and showed her passport to the receptionist. Detective Bondi did the same before a single room key is given over.

Anonasai and Detective Bondi looked at each other aghast, then back at the receptionist.

'No, not together,' conveyed Anonasai.

'Sorry, there is only one room left.'

Anonasai turned away from the front desk and looked around. She noticed three cameras turn and point to the front desk. She sighed in defeat and took the offered key. Detective Bondi followed her to the elevator.

'Ah, what was that about?'

'Three cameras in reception. One face recognition, two normal. The receptionist was stalling.'

'How do you know that?'

'Facial recognition cameras came out in 1946. Most had a remodel in 1966 to look like normal cameras. They are an eyesore if you know what you are looking for.'

Detective Bondi thought about this information. He did see three cameras but not a facial one.

'But how do you know this?'

'Two words, Makino clan.'

The elevator dings before opening to the fourth floor. Detective Bondi scanned the key card into the assigned door.

'Why are you here anyway, Miss Kaisøn?'

'You're a detective. Figure it out.'

Detective Bondi rubbed the back of his neck before closing the front door, then muttered to himself, 'First, she takes my phone and then tells me how to do my job – great start to the day.'

Anonasai entered the bedroom and froze as she saw an envelope on the queen-sized bed. On the envelope was a purple heart with a red slash through it. She opened the letter to see a map and directions. *A Makino clan meeting? Out here? The Makino are localised, not widespread.*

She put her sports bag under the bed, took out her mask, hid it in her black jumper, and left.

'Leaving already? We just got here.'

She said nothing as she left. The detective walked into the bedroom to see a letter and thought nothing of it. *Perhaps she didn't like the bathroom and went to find a better one.*

So Anonasai left the apartment and walked out of the hotel. She proceeded to the throughfare and followed the directions she had memorised to an old theatre. There was a white bucket full of nails at the theatre's entrance, so she took a handful and walked inside. Anonasai walked towards the stage and took in what remained of the grand theatre. Rows of red velvet seats were once filled with an audience looking in awe as performers stood on the polished stage. Now all that was left was the stage and moth-eaten curtains. Some of the velvet chairs had gathered mould spots; others were threadbare and perishing. Cobwebs and mould lined the walls, and plaster on the ceiling began to give way to gravity.

She began tapping the nails on a white ring around her right index finger; she stretched the nails longer and sharper until she was happy.

Five minutes later, the wooden doors creaked open and masked men filed in. Anonasai put on her mask.

A distorted male voice spoke. 'Ah, Anonasai, the wandering assassin — princess of the Makino clan — you came.'

'You gave me no choice,' replied Anonasai gruffly.

'There are always choices.'

Anonasai leapt onto the stage, the wood creaking under

her weight. From here she saw six masked men walking down the centre aisle. Two men at each exit. Three men stood in the centre aisle with a hostage. Their hostage had a black bag over his head and a torn suit. Twelve people in total. Anonasai smiled to herself — she liked these odds.

The hostage was walked five rows down and forced into a putrefied chair. The third man standing a row behind drew a gun and held it against the hostage's head.

'You, Anonasai, were the princess of the clan. You had us, your followers, at your feet. Then one day, you vanished. So, we… we had to join The Head. We couldn't do the errands we used to.'

'So, this is how you call upon your so-called princess. By summoning her with a letter.' Anonasai scoffed, then continued, 'You do remember I hate letters! The Head knows that, Sax.'

'I'm honoured you remembered me, truly I am. There is just one problem with contacting you.'

'What's that?'

'You never did give me your number.'

Anonasai rolled her eyes and tucked her hands into her jacket pockets, fidgeting with her nails.

'Get to the point, Sax,' ordered Anonasai.

'You left us behind! But … we found you at the airport with this man.'

Sax stood in the centre of the theatre with a gold band

around his left arm and waved to his companions to his right.

With the black bag removed, Kotoshi Hyosuke looked around to see the old and decaying room. First, he saw the masked men, then his eyes were drawn to her. Standing upon the stage was Anonasai with her mask on. He wasn't gagged, just tied up.

'What is this?' hissed Anonasai.

'You're smart. Figure it out,' countered a masked man.

'Idiot,' said Hyosuke.

Seconds later, the masked man standing beside Hyosuke, fell lifeless. The masked man behind Hyosuke looked at his fallen comrade and a small puddle of blood pooling from his neck before seeing a long, nail-like object. Anonasai stood with her arms crossed, sharp objects protruding between her fingers.

'Hey, what are you holding?' yelled Sax.

'Something I picked up outside. Be careful about what you say,' warned Anonasai.

'What happens if we don't?' whispered a subordinate at an exit.

'You'll end up like John Doe.'

'You, you would kill your followers?' screeched Sax.

'As you said, Sax, you joined The Head. My followers, my true followers, still follow me. Those who join and follow The Head are my enemies. They don't wear ridiculous bands on their arms.'

'It's a leader's band! No one follows you. You're an outcast!' yelled Sax.

'That is where you are wrong. I still have followers in the Makino,' disclosed Anonasai as she laughed without mirth.

'Sax, we should leave,' whispered Sax's right guard.

'No, we still have an ace up our sleeve. Know your place,' replied Sax.

Anonasai looked at Hyosuke as the gunman cocked his firearm.

'Release Kotoshi Hyosuke and you'll leave alive. If not, you have your instructions. You know the rest.'

'Hunting Bird, forget about me. I have made my peace.'

'You heard him,' replied Sax.

'That wasn't for you,' hissed Anonasai.

Anonasai lowered her head slightly as her irises turned white.

CHAPTER 4

Anonasai threw six long nails, spraying them across the theatre. One clogged the barrel of the gun and another ripped the gunman's throat leaving him gurgling. The last four nails travelled fast and true, taking out the guards next to Sax and Hyosuke. Before anyone could take a breath, the guards fell, lifeless, as she hurtled like a blur towards Sax. Hyosuke freed himself and took cover under the old seats. He took a long nail from one of the fallen and threw it at another masked Makino clan member, piercing his windpipe. A guard at the right exit ran forward and swung at Anonasai. She dodged left and kicked him into the wall.

Three more nails flew into the necks of the last three guards as she neared Sax. Sax pulled out a knife from his jacket. Anonasai blocked the blade before cracking Sax's head across her left knee. Hyosuke ran from the centre aisle and appeared behind Sax, blinded in pain. From behind, Anonasai was taken by surprise as a follower put her in a head lock. She looked around for aid only to see Hyosuke had his hands full.

Soon all the fighting stopped as a gunshot echoed out.

Anonasai slammed her foot down on one of the followers. In her rage she lodged a nail in his windpipe. She ignored the follower's gurgles as he struggled for air, and she kicked Sax away from Hyosuke before she saw Detective Bondi standing at the left exit. Bondi fired again as a Makino member rushed at him with a knife. Sax had surrounded the place with his goons. *That's surprisingly smart of him*, thought Anonasai.

Sax elbowed Hyosuke in the face, so Anonasai kneed him as hard as she could in the stomach. He splattered and puked blood; it poured out of his mouth and nose before Anonasai kicked him to the west side of the theatre.

'What the bloody hell is going on here?' asked Detective Bondi.

Before Detective Bondi got an answer, he had to dodge a body as it flew at him and into the wall headfirst. Sax fell to the ground and didn't move as debris fell on his body. 'Is he? … Did you just kill a man!?'

'No, he was just using his head,' replies Hyosuke as he walked up the stairs holding his bleeding nose.

Anonasai gathered all of her long nails, retrieving them one by one before walking over to Detective Bondi.

Detective Bondi asked, 'What happened?'

'It's best you don't know, Noah,' replied Hyosuke.

'Officer Kotoshi Hyosuke, why are you here? Last I heard, you were back in Japan.'

Hyosuke looked at Bondi with uncertainty, wondering how he had found them.

'Detective Bondi, are you keeping tabs on Silverfox?' questioned Anonasai.

'No, no, nothing of the sort,' replied Detective Bondi defensively.

'I never made it back to Japan. I got err … jumped at the airport and was taken to a warehouse.'

Noah went pale as a phone pinged. Anonasai looked at Sax's body before walking over.

'Noah, who told you I made it to Japan?'

'It was a friend of mine in the forces. You got off the plane in Tokyo.'

Detective Bondi looked at Anonasai as she neared the body and moved the leather jacket to access his phone.

'*YOU* can't loot a dead person. That's …'

'Leave her, Anonasai is getting answers.'

'You, Detective Bondi, have no jurisdiction here,' declared Anonasai.

Detective Bondi looked at Hyosuke, defeated, before realising the situation. 'Neither do you! You're just a citizen at a crime scene.'

'Anonasai, respect the dead and leave them. We must go now before local law enforcements arrive,' ordered Hyosuke.

Anonasai looked at Hyosuke and frowned. She hated being ordered around, but she followed him out of the theatre. Detective Bondi stayed at the scene as police cars arrived at the location shortly after.

Detective Bondi relayed the details, helping police write up their reports. They went over every little detail multiple times so as not to miss a thing. Before he arrived back at the hotel, the sun had set and the streetlights had turned on.

When Noah opened the door to the apartment, he saw Anonasai looking out the window and Hyosuke sleeping on the bed. He walked over to the coffee machine and made a cup of coffee. 'I'm guessing you saw everything then?'

'Yes. You work for MI5.'

Noah froze mid-step. 'Ah … no, I'm just a detective.'

'It's not wise to lie to me.'

Anonasai closed the curtains and she turned on the television. Noah read his information on the television screen and took a sip of coffee.

Name: Noah J. Bondi

Rank: Agent

Country: United Kingdom

Sex: Male

Mother: Classified

Age: Classified

Father: Classified

Blood type: O+

Eye Colour: Blue

Hair Colour: Brown

Address: Classified

Weapons: Classified

Vehicles: Full access

Assignment: Find and apprehend the wandering assassin/ Hunting Bird.

Assist: Classified

'You hacked into the MI5 mainframe?' said Noah in disbelief.

'That's the least of your worries.'

Noah looked at Hyosuke once more then at his coffee mug before seeing scuff marks on the floor.

'Before the Mickey Finn knocks you out, how exactly would you have apprehended me?'

'A spy doesn't reveal his secrets.'

'Well, a drugged beverage may surprise the unsuspected like Hyosuke, but for me, you need to be more creative.'

'How so?' asked Noah.

'Sorry, a wandering assassin doesn't reveal her secrets. Not to MI5 or detectives. Are you alone on this mission?'

'Does Hyosuke know?' Noah began to slur his words.

'Know what?'

'About your past and what you have done.'

'You are stalling, and that's not going to help you. Are you alone?' she repeated.

Before Noah answered, he fell to the floor in a heap. The coffee cup smashed into pieces. Anonasai clicked her tongue before dragging Noah to a nearby closet where he would sleep it off. She cleaned up the mess and then looked at the coffee pot. It had been centuries since she had last slept. So, she opened her sports bag, put her weapons inside, and poured the last part of the drugged coffee into a cup. She looked at the brown liquid; she saw her reflection and something else – her green eyes with the hint of brown. She looked closer to see a small wood and mortar home with a red cross. *Did I dare drink it?* She thought back to when she last slept, but the thought never came forward. *Had it really been that long? No, I nearly fell into slumber at the airport before ... that officer put a gun to my head, but prior to that ... it had been too long.* Screams entered her head. People were screaming, and the smell of smoke and burning flesh choked her.

A tear fell into her reflection, bringing her back to reality. Anonasai watched the small ripple before pouring the coffee down the sink. She cleaned the coffee pot and mug before walking to a small desk near the window and opening a black laptop. She saw the latest news about the Republic of Telfax.

Food and water in rations; hospitals being bombed; people killed in their homes because the enemy believed they were army personnel. So, she brought up her map of Telfax and the Escaian Army. She saw the way the war was heading — saw the circle. She sent an encrypted email to the prime minister of Telfax. *'Implement a tactic now before another city is lost, or the capital.'*

Her brother had the golden mace of the house. She just had to get it back. So, she contacted the only follower she trusted in the Makino clan. She called the secured line with this follower, and it opened.

'Anonasai? Is that you?' whispered a female voice.

'Yes, Ping, it's me. I need you to find an item for me.'

'A recon, how exciting. What is this item?'

'The Republic of Telfax Golden Mace of the House.'

'But The Head has that in his...'

'I know. Could you get it? Once you do, send a photo to Telfax's PM.'

'I understand. Once I have it, what do I do with it?'

'Well, the mace can't be sent overseas, it'll be confiscated.'

The line went quiet for a few moments before Anonasai continued. 'Airdrop it.'

'You can't be serious! A multi-million-dollar item dead-dropped out of a plane?'

'I am. It's the only way to get it back to the Telfaxian prime minister without others knowing.'

'Surely we can have our people run it to him,' suggested Ping.

'Sax and his men attacked me today.'

'And Sax?'

'Didn't make it.'

'Oh, Anonasai …' Ping sounded sympathetic before getting right back to business. 'What's the location?'

'Just inside the Telfaxian border.'

'I know. Escaian forces at this time are not around.'

'I hope so. I can't help my end.'

'I know. Thank you, Ping.'

'Be safe and live, Anonasai.'

'And you, Ping.'

Anonasai hung up with a smile as she planned a safe journey to the drop-off zone. She emailed the prime minister of Telfax about her plan. His response was instant. *Good, he had been seeing my emails.* His silence was a worry, but she would meet up with him or a soldier in three days at the border with a package.

Now her mission would begin to assassinate the Escaian figurehead before then. She researched possible spots the figurehead would be hidden and possible escape routes, but she just had to locate her target for now. She studied other figurehead meetings with her target and media reports until they led her to one building. *The media may be false and sometimes repetitive, but it is handy. For example, the white stone house with golden domes. Red-brick walls lined the outer perimeter with barbed-wire fastened to the top. This must be my target.* Anonasai smiled as she hacked into Ecsay's city records to pull up blueprints to find out if the building had a bunker and tunnels. She planned for mishaps, but one mishap she would have to deal with soon was in the closet. *Was he going to get in my way? Or was he going to work with me? Could I trust Noah? No, he lied to me. However, that was his job to continue his mission as a spy now that he was found out.* She rolled her eyes as she studied the blueprints.

Noah Bondi wasn't her problem. Once the Mickey Finn wore off, she planned to get rid of him, and that headache would be over. Dawn was approaching, and soon her plan would be put into action. A notice popped up on her laptop screen. She glanced at it to see an encryption. She clicked on it. It was from Ping: *I have it, sent a photo to the PM of Telfax. En route to the location.*

CHAPTER 5

Kotoshi Hyosuke prised his eyes open and squinted at the twilight room. His body felt heavy and the dimly lit room aggravated his dull headache. The last thing he heard was people mumbling, then footsteps approached him. He felt icy cold fingers wrapped around his right wrist, checking for a pulse; *how charming, but the bone-chilling touch was unbearable.* Memories of the warehouse flashed into his mind. Being pushed so far to the edge that the knockouts were blissful ... then there was the frozen water poured over him to wake him up. Left in his wet, torn clothing before turning on the heater; *no, not again.* He saw a shadow beside him preoccupied with his hand, so he quickly grabbed the bedside table lamp and threw it, only it was caught.

'Still as agile as ever, even after being drugged I see.'

'My apologies, Hunting Bird.'

Anonasai put the jade lamp back before lighting up the room. Hyosuke felt relieved, as he saw his torn suit was still on. He sat up to see no indication of a break-in; *even if someone broke in, they would have to deal with her and…*

'Where is Noah?' enquired Hyosuke.

'Don't worry about him. He is sleeping off the Mickey Finn as well.'

'As well … how?'

'It was in the coffee,' disclosed Anonasai.

The coffee of course would mask such a drug. Someone else knows she is here and now they would have to be diligent, more so than ever. 'Why didn't it affect you? Did you not drink?'

'No, you collapsed before I drank.'

Hyosuke looked around the room once more before an explosion lit up the dawning sky. The sonic boom rumbled softly as it was miles away.

'Why are you here in a war zone?'

Anonasai didn't answer at first, so Hyosuke moved to sit on the edge of the bed and asked, 'What is it?'

'Sax the Makino had you in their hands. They were ready to kill you.'

'Your brother is a mighty man. He didn't like it when I infiltrated his ranks using his sister, and you dishonoured your mask.'

Anonasai smiled and sighed, 'Mm … that was thirty years ago. He needs to let that go.'

'It hurt him. Family is a powerful bond.'

'Yes, yes, but it was fun.'

'Which part?'

'When your fellow officers were discussing your plan. Then your party wasn't expecting a woman to enter that room.'

'I wasn't expecting my officers to go for you like that and for you to retaliate.'

Anonasai crossed her arms, saying, 'It was my room, after all. Also, you weren't wearing masks, so I knew you were intruders.'

'It was kind of you not to alert anyone, considering your reputation.'

'Yes, well, you have Court to thank for that.'

'Court? Your hacker?'

'Yes.'

A thud echoed from the closet. Hyosuke looked over his shoulder before reaching for his gun. He looked at the bedside table to see it was missing.

'Under the bed.'

Anonasai walked without caution, opening the closet door and watching as Noah tumbled out with his hands and feet tied.

'Why were you in there?' questioned Hyosuke.

'I'm guessing you put me in the closet?' replied Noah looking at Anonasai.

Anonasai smiled, then crouched down. 'I'd hoped you would bite your tongue.'

'Anonasai, what did you do?' Hyosuke sounded alarmed.

'Did you know that Detective Bondi works for MI5? Or that he is assigned to capture me?'

Hyosuke nodded before walking around the bed to stand with Anonasai. Detective Bondi sat and looked up at them both.

'So, the drug was supposed to capture her?' asked Hyosuke.

'Yes, only you weren't supposed to be here,' answered Noah with a strange accent.

'Do you know what happens to people that cross her path?' Hyosuke continued.

'She kills them. I know I read that. Listen, Agent Bondi got in too deep.'

'Bondi, you're Bondi, aren't you?' queried Anonasai with a confused expression.

Hyosuke looked at Anonasai and then at the man sitting before them, who moved his neck to show a wire. Hyosuke fired his gun at the man's feet, making him jump. 'I'll ask once ... who are you?'

'Zino Koloife. A group of men smuggled me off the street to replace an Englishman. I ... was told about a man named Bondi and to agree to everything said by you two.'

Anonasai stepped closer to Zino and he flinched.

'He's telling the truth. These men, what did they look like?'

'One looked like me. I didn't see the other two.' Zino kept looking down at his chest.

'So, Zino, you don't know who snatched you off the street?' asked Anonasai as she looked at his chest.

'He's innocent,' announced Hyosuke.

'No one is innocent,' snapped Zino.

'I was thirty years ago,' replied Anonasai solemnly.

Hyosuke narrowed his brow at Anonasai and looked at Zino before asking, 'Will you talk?'

'No.'

Anonasai smirked then looked at Hyosuke then at her sports bag. He understood the gesture and slid it to her. She opened it and pulled out winter gear and a map of Europe. Then she placed her hand on a scanner. A false compartment turned over, revealing guns, knives and her mask. Finally, she signalled Hyosuke to keep Zino talking as she put on her mask.

'What were you doing on the street before being smuggled, Zino?' asked Hyosuke.

'I was walking home from my mother's house. I wanted to make sure she was okay after an explosion hit her area.'

Anonasai cut off the restraints before cutting Zino's shirt off halfway. She saw wires and a round object wrapped in tin foil on a vest.

'When I got to her house, it was a mess. Bricks, glass and ash were everywhere. I called Ma's name. I screamed and screamed until a neighbour told me she had left hours before.'

Anonasai cut a red wire before examining the vest further. She saw two more round objects.

'Stay still,' ordered Anonasai in a distressed voice.

Hyosuke and Zino looked at her as she cut a blue wire. The room froze as if nothing had happened. Zino hugged Anonasai before quickly getting the suit and vest off then heading for the door. Before Zino could fully leave the apartment, Hyosuke grabbed his arm and asked, 'How did you get into the closet?'

'There is a false back,' Zino whispered.

Anonasai ripped open the closet door and looked for a hinge or a hole. But Hyosuke pulled Anonasai aside and fired at the back boarding. As shards of wood flew, a chilled wind exited from the spot, and Zino slipped out of the apartment. Hyosuke kicked the back of the closet in and revealed a surveillance room. The previous occupants had left empty food wrappings, wires, alcohol bottles and five monitors. Anonasai headed for the door that led into the hallway while Hyosuke analysed the monitors.

On the monitors, Hyosuke saw the hallway, the bedroom, kitchen; the other two monitors were for personal use, under the name of Rem Hitchcock.

So, Hyosuke looked into this Rem Hitchcock to learn that he was an American and was now stationed in Europe. He started to look at the footage saved when it began one day ago. It showed Anonasai and Noah in the room. There was a letter on the bed. She read the letter and hid her sports bag before leaving. Noah was on the phone within seconds;

two people entered from the closet. A woman walked over to the kitchen before stepping back into view, saying to Noah, 'Don't drink anything, you'll have a headache. If you do, we'll bring an undercover in to replace you. We'll strap a vest with gasses onto its chest.' Noah asked, 'What's on the vest?' The woman replied, 'Nothing lethal, just something to knock her out.' The male added, 'If you must know, Propofol.' The two agents re-entered the closet.

Anonasai watched the hall as Hyosuke continued to watch the screen. He saw himself drinking the laced coffee. He looked closely at the screen as he fell and that Anonasai didn't drink. He saw her leave her cup on the table, rush over to him and check his pulse before heading to her bag. She put a dipstick into her drink and waited before the results showed. Then he saw Anonasai carrying his unconscious body to the bed.

'Hyosuke, we need to go. A woman in a suit is heading this way.'

But he didn't hear her. So Anonasai closed the door, pulled Hyosuke away from the monitors and into the apartment.

'How long have you been here?' asked Hyosuke.

'Two days.'

'You have been followed. Noah and three others know you are here. Zino collaborates with them. They are working together to …'

'Capture me, I know, but I have work to do.'

'Anonasai.'

'Don't tell me you're going to stop me.'

Hyosuke placed his black dragon weapon on the left bedside table before crossing his arms.

'You are here, on this land, during a war. VIPs go into bunkers or under heavy guard. You can't just walk in and kill them.'

'I already have a plan for that.'

'What is it?'

'I've been sending tactics to the opposing side. So far, it's working.'

Hyosuke narrowed his eyes as the building shook.

'Every country wants you in prison or dead, so how did you get the Republic of Telfax to listen to you?'

'I told them the truth in exchange for their Golden Mace of the House.'

'Who has it?'

'My brother.'

Hyosuke unfolded his arms as Anonasai entered the hallway. Hyosuke followed her, one door down, where Anonasai knocked and waited. The brown door opened slowly. Anonasai recognised the female agent and kicked the door wide open.

The woman reached behind her back, but Hyosuke ran in and subdued her.

'Wait, wait, I'm not here to do anything.'

'Don't speak false words. You drugged the coffee and sent Zino into the apartment,' hissed Hyosuke.

'Yes, we did that, but we only wanted to talk to the wandering assassin.'

'A simple, *hello can we talk?* would've been nice. Surely manners and etiquette haven't dissipated over the years,' mocked Anonasai.

The woman looked confused as Hyosuke searched the room for something to tie the spy's hands. Soon enough, he found zip ties nearby and used them. Hyosuke walked in front of the female spy once more and leaned on the kicked-in door. 'No one uses the word etiquette anymore.'

'Go, I can handle things here,' Hyosuke ensured Anonasai.

Anonasai stared down the brown-haired American. She looked at her friend with concern before leaving and taking the elevator. She exited the elevator thirty seconds later into the reception foyer only to face Agent Bondi with one of his colleagues.

Noah was dumbstruck.

Agent Sharp looked at his colleague. 'Bondi?'

'Yeah, I know, I see her.'

'New friend, agent or another person you smuggled off the street?' Anonasai smugly asked.

Agent Bondi smiled and walked towards Anonasai, who headed for the front entrance. Agent Sharp intercepted her and blocked her way.

'Funny, I'm guessing you and Silverfox found Remmy.'

Anonasai smirked. 'Yes, we did. Better hurry, foxes like to rip birds apart.'

'Bondi, what is she talking about?' asked Agent Sharp.

'She's bluffing,' Noah assured him.

Anonasai stopped her advance and crossed her arms. Sharp looked at Bondi and the woman in front of him before drawing his 9mm Glock. Citizens in the foyer hiding from missiles quickly took cover behind armchairs and turned side tables over, fearing for their safety.

'Easy, Sharp,' said Bondi, trying to keep the situation calm.

Anonasai smiled. 'So, Bondi, you are in charge of him? Do yourself a favour, Agent Sharp, and put the gun away, as a ricochet from a bullet would kill a civilian.'

Agent Sharp sighed in defeat before declaring, 'Bondi isn't in charge of me.'

'Good.' Anonasai walked past the agents to the front door and left.

'I hate that woman,' stated Agent Sharp under his breath.

'Join the club. Let's go save Remmy.'

Agents Sharp and Bondi took the elevator up to the fourth floor and ran to their surveillance room to find Remmy tied to a chair with red wires and gagged with a white cloth.

'What happened? Who did this?' asked Sharp as he removes the gag out of her mouth.

'The man aiding our suspect. Don't worry, I'm not hurt by

the way. Please tell me you have them in a different room and rushed to check on me.'

The two agents look at each other, then back at Remmy.

'No, they both got away,' admitted Noah.

'Well, shit! Kotoshi Hyosuke said little,' disclosed Remmy.

'He spoke to you?' asked Sharp, releasing Remmy from the wires and zip ties.

'Yes, I am pretty, after all.'

'Remmy, what did he say?' demanded Agent Sharp with impatience.

'*Don't follow her* ... then he touched the computers. My computers! Can you believe that?!'

The three agents looked at each other before rushing over to the computers.

'Why didn't you say that first?' snapped Agent Sharp.

'Shut up and look for anything that is missing,' hissed Noah.

After searching and running several diagnostics, they discovered three files had been copied to an unknown source.

'Shit, all our intel on her was copied. Command will not like this,' moaned Remmy.

'Command doesn't need to know. We need to get our hands on Kotoshi Hyosuke and the copies he made.'

'How? You said on the walk over here that they're both ghosts,' queried Sharp.

'Anonasai is not. She doesn't know how to hide.'

'How are you going to get close to her now? Our cover has been blown, and there is no way she will trust you again,' conveyed Remmy.

Remmy hacked into the Escaian cameras to see traffic and citizens fleeing, fires in the streets and buildings, and armed forces of Escya moving over the Republic of Telfax border.

'She is the wandering assassin. We both have the same target. But I have to protect the guy. I'm sure she is pursuing him.'

'If so, Noah, how are you, or how are we, apprehending her?'

'We will set a lead for her to follow and send out false reports that our target is in …'

Rem pulled up a network of the Escaian Embassy and put together false reports before posting them on media outlets.

'Do you have a backup plan, Remmy? Unfortunately, they didn't work back home.'

'I wasn't planning on that truck, or planning for her quick driving skills!'

'That's why I drive,' replied Agent Sharp.

'No one drives my cars anymore. You trashed the last Banshee Chevrolet Camaro 5000 we had. I loved that car,' snapped Remmy.

Noah left the room before Remmy could go all car lover on him again. He entered the elevator and waited. Agent Sharp soon dashed in. 'She's giving you the talk again?'

'Yep, a clean car is a good car … blah blah … who eats in a car anyway?'

The elevator soon opened on the ground floor and they walked from the reception to the street. Both agents crossed the road to their silver charger. Agent Sharp unlocked the car as they were halfway across the street with a Bluetooth sensor. His attention was soon caught by an illumination in a puddle under the car.

'Noah, did it rain last night?'

'No, I don't think so. Why?'

Agent Sharp focused on the puddle. He noticed a small blinking red light.

'Noah, the car!'

Noah knew what that meant. They raced away as the silver charger exploded. Glass shattered, becoming projectiles as the shockwaves blew out nearby windows. Debris littered the street as the vehicle burned. Nearby car alarms blared as they were rocked from the blast.

Noah looked around him as his ears rang. Hands grabbed his shoulders, picking him up from the ground. He looked around at the individual who aided him to his feet. *Dan. Good, my colleague is alive, but what about Remmy?*

'Rem, Remmy, where is Remmy?'

'Remmy is getting what she can and meeting us soon.'

Noah released himself from Sharp's grip and stood.

'What the hell was that? A car bomb!' yelled Noah, unaware

of his volume.

'We need to follow protocol. We need to meet up with Remmy at the second safe house,' hissed Agent Sharp.

Noah looked at the sky in time to see three fighter jets roar past. The two agents ran to their second safe house. It was a little white-brick house five blocks from the main streets. Agent Sharp knocked on the iron door with the help of the door knocker.

Remmy opened the door to see her comrades and hurried them inside.

Remmy started, 'What the hell did you do to my car?'

'Don't start with that bullshit again,' snapped Noah.

'We're fine, thank you.' Agent Sharp looked at Noah to see dried blood on his collar and his ears.

Remmy scanned Noah from head to toe with a wand in her right hand while she held a tablet in her left. 'Eh, just a concussion. You will be fine.'

'A concussion can be serious,' moaned Noah.

'So, how were you able to run?'

Agent Sharp handed Noah a white tablet with a glass of water before looking at Remmy, stating, 'There must be something wrong with that medical device. Besides, why was there a bomb under the car?'

'I'm looking into that. As far as reports go, Escya believes the Republic of Telfax is behind the car bomb.'

Agent Sharp looked at the monitors that Rem had set up

to view a live camera feed. Red squares framed civilians' faces. A camera scanned for their target while another secured their location.

'Where is our target?' enquired Noah.

'Which one? The assassin or the figurehead?' questioned Remmy.

'The figurehead. I can just handcuff her.'

'Why didn't you then, when you saw her in that alley or the apartment,' scoffed Sharp.

'I wanted to have a little fun.'

'Sure, getting drugged and nearly getting blown up is fun,' answered Remmy sarcastically.

'Or getting your face smashed in. How is her hand not broken? She smashed those bricks like they were made of butter and can still operate her hand,' added Agent Sharp with seriousness.

Noah shrugged his shoulders as a computer locked onto a civilian.

Remmy enlarged the image to see a black-haired woman in black clothing. Her hoodie failed to hide her face. Agent Sharp and Noah walked over to see.

'That's her,' confirmed Noah.

'I'm not getting any results from any department.'

'She's traveling under the name Miss Kaisøn. It has a line through the o.'

Remmy typed in Miss Kaisøn's name through multiple

departments with zero results.

'Sorry, she doesn't exist. Are you sure that's our target?' questioned Remmy.

'Yes, that's her, I won't forget her face any time soon,' confirmed Noah.

Sharp looked at them with a raised eyebrow. 'Miss Kaisøn is an alias then. It looks like we get to question her after all. Remmy, where is she going?'

Remmy glared at Agent Sharp before saying, 'Do you remember our mission or not? We are not to talk to her.'

'Why? I'm an interrogator. If I'm not interrogating anyone, why am I here?'

'Just follow the mission orders, Agent Sharp,' hissed Remmy.

'My mission is to talk to Anonasai when Agent Noah Bondi apprehends her.'

Remmy stared at Dan then at Noah. Finally, she moved away from her computers to the middle of the room.

'What? Why is that a shock to you?' asked Agent Bondi.

'I was told that Agent Bondi and Agent Sharp are to protect someone from being assassinated. You two are to capture the assassin then we go home. No questioning, no hiccups. In and out. I'm the driver, the hacker and the planner.'

'Sorry, love, but some information was kept from you by MI5. Can't have everyone knowing,' replied Agent Bondi as he dressed into Escaian formal wear. It was a black tuxedo with white underlay. On his right arm was an armband with an Escaian flag emblazoned on it.

'I made you IDs that will get you in, but everything else is up to you. I hope you have been practising your Escaian,' said Remmy.

'Yeah, I know a few key points.'

Remmy walked away from Agent Bondi looking worried. 'We're doomed.'

'Safe word?' asked Agent Sharp.

'Makino.'

'No, if you see her, she will know,' suggested Dan.

'How about *idiot* because you look and sound like one!' grumbled Remmy as she typed away.

Noah winced. 'Fine.'

Noah walked out to an unmarked bus that was to take him back into the city. Remmy stood with her arms crossed as she watched the black bus getting smaller and smaller.

'A moment of silence for the big *idiot*.'

Agent Sharp pushed Remmy aside before walking inside.

'I'm pretty sure that's against the law here.'

'Then I'll shoot whoever saw me. Besides this area is secluded.'

CHAPTER 6

Anonasai walked the streets of asphalt while looking at maps to find a greyed-out area nearby. All she saw were red-brick walls. She was close. She walked around the east side of the brick wall to the north before ducking back. Four guards stood at the entrance in teal uniforms. She looked around the corner again to see the guards busy with a black bus. To say the least, it wasn't a tourist bus, so this must be a workers' bus.

She hid in small bushes and trees just around the corner again as yelling echoed. If someone came to her location, it wouldn't be enough to conceal her.

In the distance a voice is heard saying, 'Sorry, I just have to get this.'

'No, no phone calls!!' yelled a cantankerous guard.

'I'll only be quick.'

Anonasai knew that voice. She quickly looked at her surroundings again, the bushes wouldn't hide her so she ran to the tree and hid as footsteps crunched on pebbles approaching the eastern wall.

'Hello?'

'Noah, are you in yet?' It was Remmy's voice.

'I would be if you didn't call me!' hissed Noah with irritation.

'Sorry, your tracker lost connection.'

'Does everything else work?'

'Yes.'

'Then I'm bloody fine!' snapped Noah, then he hung up and pocketed his phone. He sighed as a knife is pressed against his throat.

'Lyogkyi [easy],' Noah says in Escaian.

'So, you are protecting the figurehead.'

'Are you here to stop me, Anonasai?'

Agent Bondi quickly grabbed her right hand and threw her at the brick wall. Her body bounced off but she lost her knife in the grass. Before she could regain her footing, he pulled her up by her throat. Anonasai's eyes turn white as she stared him down. His grip grew tighter and tighter until her larynx snapped.

'Mr Kolofski, we will not wait any longer!' yelled a soldier.

Noah released his hold on Anonasai and watched her slide down to the soft green grass before falling left without a sound. Agent Bondi straightened his suit and walked back to the north entrance where he proceeded through the front gate.

CHAPTER 7

While lying unconscious, old memories came forth. It was cold and dark. The sky was lifeless, not a star or moon in sight. The streets were cobblestone and dirt, and the smell of days-old urine and faeces left under house windows made her screw up her nose. Anonasai looked around at the wood and mortar homes. They looked familiar. This was her home; these streets were hers. She walked down the cobblestone road to a wooden house with a red cross on the door. She opened the door to see her mother and father decomposing. Their red hair thinned out; their eyes closed but caved in. Her mother was in her favourite white dress with dried lavender and rosemary sewn into it; now stained with death. Her father's clothes, a white T-shirt, a green vest, and cream pants, were also stained with death.

Her knees buckled, making her fall into a puddle of vinegar

at the house's entrance. Tears flowed down her cheeks as she silently wept. Warm hands touched her shoulders before leading her away from the dead.

'You shouldn't have seen that. I'm sorry.'

'Was it the plague?' she asked.

'Yes, I'm sorry.'

'My brother wasn't there. Where is he?'

'Constantine? Don't worry, he is by the River Thames. He is looking for you. We all were.'

She ran as fast as possible to the riverbank. She yelled his name repeatedly until someone hugged her from behind and said, 'Shut up, I'm right behind you.'

'Constantine!'

'Anna, I'm glad you're safe.'

It was too dark to see his features; she could see his white shirt and purple vest, but she knew it was him by his voice and the awful smell of rosemary and vinegar.

'I saw them … saw Mother and Father.'

'I know I saw as well. I … uh, hoped it wasn't true.'

'What now?'

'Well, we stay together and head out into the world.'

Anonasai released herself from his grip and turned to see his silhouette.

'With what? We have no money. We don't have papers. We need papers to travel, and where will we go?'

'Do not fret, sister. I work for the king. All I need is three days. A royal doctor will see us, and we can travel wherever we want,' reassured Constantine.

Anonasai was silent for too long as the night sky lightened to a soft purple then to blue. She saw her brother; his red hair was combed back and his emerald-green eyes were focussed on her. His pale skin darkened to a soft tan as the sun rose.

'I know this plague worries you more now than ever. So, let's run from it. Let's ...'

'You can't run from disease. You can only control it,' hissed Anna, crossing her arms.

'I know, as you have said a thousand times, which is why the king and council ordered culling cats and dogs.'

Anna walked to Constantine and stood beside him. 'What about the rats and mice?'

Constantine looked at Anna. 'What about them?'

'Sure, kill all the cats and dogs, but rats and mice are still in the thousands. They can still enter our homes. For all we know, they could be spreading the plague.'

'Anna, you can't believe this.'

'You and I are smart. That's why you protect the king. Work for the king. While I do my work.'

'You work as a historian.'

'That is why we know many things. The culling of cats and dogs did nothing. The plague is still spreading. That is why we need to cull the rats and mice.'

Constantine breathed in the morning air and thought the

information over before grabbing his sister's hand, then ran up the banks of the Thames to the street. He waved for a carriage to stop.

'Constantine, where are we going?'

'You're going to tell the king what you just told me.'

She ripped her hand from Constantine's before hissing, 'Excuse me, meet the king? Tell King Charles II? No thank you.'

'Why not? It will be revolutionary. Think about it … you will help thousands of people.'

'Listen to yourself. Women do little work. I do my work in secret. Therefore, I cannot meet the king. Relay my information if you must. Lie if you must.'

'Lie? Lie to the king. I will be killed.'

'Then don't tell the king.'

A carriage stopped in front of Constantine and Anna; the coachman opened the door and waited for his new patrons to board. Constantine looked at Anna before giving her a letter.

'Meet me at Mother and Father's place tonight.'

'And if not?'

'River Thames!' yelled Constantine as the carriage moved away.

Anna looked at the letter in her hand to see her name written elegantly. Her mother's handwriting. She stared at the letter before a single tear fell next to her name. She focused on the water stain before collecting herself.

She didn't open it, not yet. Instead, she walked around

London as people went about their day. She was good at avoiding windows and people, exceptionally good at it. Before she went to the River Thames, she grabbed a shawl from a crowded stall, then walked to the riverbank and sat there. She watched the small waves lap the shore and breathed in the salty air. Listening to the waves, she closed her eyes.

'Anna, Anna. ANNA!'

Anna opened her eyes abruptly. A male was shaking her, so she punched him in the jaw. He fell to the sand holding the right side of his jaw.

'Easy, easy, it's Constantine.'

'Sorry, I told you to never sneak up on me like that.'

'I thought you were dead.'

Anna stood up and brushed sand from her legs.

'Did you check my heartbeat?'

'Yes, but …'

'Then I am alive, you bloody idiot.'

Anna looked at Constantine to see that the sand and his skin had an orange glow. Then she smelt it — the smell of smoke. She looked towards town to see a small fire.

'We need to leave,' said Anna with fear.

Constantine held out his right hand, and Anna took it without hesitation as they ran along the riverbank and up to a small wooden house. Constantine grabbed papers and shoved books into a leather satchel before leading Anna down an alley.

Smoke poured into the night sky, flames licked the buildings as people screamed and ran for their lives. Constantine grabbed Anna's right hand as she stared into the fire. Flames engulfed one street as Constantine pulled her away from the nightmare view. A building soon collapsed, revealing the skeletal remains of people who once lived inside.

Anna followed Constantine as they ran from the fire, smoke and screams.

'We're almost there!'

'Where?' yelled Anna.

She knew he'd yelled back, but a mysterious thundering noise behind them drowned out his answer. Her vision went black, heat engulfed them, and a black cloud choked her. She coughed and gagged on the smoke and smell of burning flesh. *Was it mine? Or was it Constantine's?*

The black cloud was never-ending. The smoke burned her throat, eyes and lungs, leaving her relatively weak. Her brother squeezed her hand harder in the darkness before pulling her down onto the hot cobblestones. The stones' heat prickled at her skin, but she could see black shoes in front of her, and ash-covered trouser legs.

The black clouds lifted and they gasped for fresh air. Her clothing was covered with ash, and so was her hair and skin. Constantine looked up at the sky to see black billowing towers of smoke and fire. Their home was surely ablaze, their town ablaze. *But how? It was a brutal winter, and the thaw out was the most challenging part with water everywhere. Had something gone wrong? Had the fire channel failed?*

Constantine looked behind his sister to see bodies lining the cobblestone road, some gasping for air, some motionless.

If they were to survive this night, Constantine had to get himself and Anna to the water, but the papers he held were essential to him and the king. Anna soon rose her head and locked eyes with him. Finally, he made up his mind. He forced himself and Anna to run again to the River Thames. That night, they waded in ankle-deep water. Anna held onto the stone wall. As Constantine stood next to Anna, his leather satchel broke and fell into the water. He quickly retrieved his bag and checked the papers inside.

'Constantine, why did we go to that little house?'

'I had to get our papers. I got ... made the king sign a doctor's certificate for you and me.'

'That's ... You can't do that!' yelled Anna.

Constantine glanced at Anna, quickly enough that it could've broken his neck. Then she heard a bone-chilling crack making her eyes shoot open.

* * *

In the twilight, she saw the green of the grass at eye level, the bushes and the brown bark of a tree. Then the smell of the dirt and grass. It had been cut four days ago. She heard birds chirping and people talking off in the distance.

Then her memory came back, a male held her by the neck, his grip getting tighter and tighter before she felt her neck crack.

I'll deal with that asshole later. I'll deal with my target first, or is my target that man? If so, that man would be lying in his blood, and I wouldn't be going through my memories.

Anonasai walked over to the bushes and saw a red sports bag peeking out from behind a tree. It looked familiar so she walked over and opened it. Inside were winter clothes and a brown passport. She flicked through a few pages to see her photo and a name, Miss Korosu Kaisøn.

Anonasai searched the bag and found a phone and headset. Her amnesia wasn't helping, so she looked in the phone to see two numbers saved. One for someone called Ping and another, Silverfox.

She called Ping first and let it ring three times before a female robotic voice answered, 'This is a secured line...' There was silence for ten seconds before another voice, 'Anonasai, you don't normally call unless something happens.'

'Ping?'

'Something's happened, hasn't it? Tell me what you remember.'

'A man, he snapped my neck. I found a red bag for Miss Korosu Kaisøn.'

'That is your bag. Listen, you are currently hunting down a figurehead in Escya.'

'Who is Anonasai?'

'You … that is your name just in case you're caught. Miss Kaisøn is your undercover name. In that bag, you'll find a hand scanner.'

She moved the clothes around to see a hand scanner and scanned her right hand. The clothes rotated to a metal compartment with a mask, guns and knives.

'I found it.'

'Good, Anonasai. Do you remember anything about how your neck broke?'

Silence, as Anonasai looked at the weapons and reached for an armour-piercing sniper bullet.

'There was this blonde man, he was on the phone. I hid this red bag. Then there was an altercation. He grabbed my neck and squeezed tighter until there was a snap.'

'Did you see your past?'

'What relevance is that?'

'Just some questions you have me ask when this happens?'

'This, this has happened before?'

'Yes, this is the second time.'

Anonasai took out the sniper bullet and looked for the rifle parts.

'I saw the sky was on fire. There was a male helping me escape.'

'Did he have a name?'

'I don't remember. He helped me, and I felt safe.'

'Did you escape? The fire?'

'Eventually.'

'How did you two become immortal?' enquired Ping.

Anonasai dropped the muzzle of the rifle in shock at the question. 'Two?'

'Yes, two.'

Anonasai looked at the weapons, the parts of firearms, and the phone. She lifted the bullet to see her reflection in gold. *Human beings can't be immortal.* Then she saw her white ring – memories flooded her mind in a flurry of images, mostly blurred.

'That will remain a mystery to you, Ping.'

Ping sighed. 'Good to have you back, Anonasai.'

'I called. Why?'

'Someone broke your neck, and you had amnesia.'

'Agent Bondi.'

'Who is Bondi?'

Anonasai took out the sniper parts from her sports bag and put the weapon together.

'A nuisance about to be put down.'

'The Head only gave you one bullet.'

She looked in her bag to see Ping was speaking the truth. One bullet for the rifle but not for the handgun.

'Thanks, Ping. I have it covered.'

'Yeah, be safe, Anonasai.'

Anonasai hung up and tied multi-functional binoculars to her hip, then packed her bag away before climbing up the tree. She climbed the tree high enough to see above the red-brick wall but not into the white building beyond, so she climbed a branch higher to see a few windows. She looked through the windows to see a few guards and housemaids. She switched to infrared. The first two floors were foot traffic to look like someone was home until a heat signature went into a dark box and disappeared downwards.

'What a pain,' hissed Anonasai.

CHAPTER 8

The blueprints that Anonasai memorised of the Escaian Embassy, with its white brick and golden domes, showed no modern technology, yet she saw it. The place still looked like a time capsule from 1833, yet technology made its way inside.

Old building with modern technology. *What a pain.* There was still a way inside the old tunnels. *Perhaps they were still open.* So, she climbed down and ran to the southern wall.

Anonasai walked close to the wall until a spotlight scanned the grounds nearby. She crouched down low against the wall and held her position as the light scanned the grass, the bushes and a small storm shelter entrance before heading towards her. The light neared, getting closer and closer before shutting off. A shout echoed as an Escaian soldier posted above yelled, 'All clear!'

'It's cold, and they are doing patrols. Why can't they drink vodka and play cards as soldiers did in the seventh world dead zones,' muttered Anonasai as she waited for the light to ascertain the intervals.

She noticed that this side of the wall was mossy and separate, unlike the west and north side, which were clean and clear. So she walked back to the southwest corner and saw no guards walking the grounds. On her way back, her hair moved like it was sucked into the wall. She looked at the wall; she couldn't see much, just the smell of moss and wine.

She stepped away when she heard a male voice coming from the moss.

'Yes, the figurehead is here. She isn't a problem anymore.'

Anonasai froze at the English accent. The wall had an opening, and she could smell wine on the wind. The spotlight soon came to life again and she watched the light as it moved along the grass to the storm shelter, the bushes, and then to the base of the wall. Finally, the light lit up the wall just enough so she could see a small gap in the moss. There was an archway covered in moss, vines and weeds.

A wine cellar: *an excellent place to talk without others listening and an excellent place to start a fire if I need it.*

The light turned on at fifteen-minute intervals. Anonasai looked around at the storm shelter. *Why is it important? The metal box wasn't attractive on the outside. Perhaps what was on the inside.* She ran over, and the light suddenly turned on.

She hid on the east side of the shelter as soldiers talked and scanned the area.

'What was that?' asked a soldier in Escaian.

'What did you see?'

'Something big — it ran across the grounds.'

'Perhaps it was a cat.'

The light went off before she reached the front and saw the decayed wood on the metal doors. The wood was rotten and she knew the hinges would be rusty and make a lot of noise. She looked back at the wall and ran back, this time not alerting the soldiers on top.

She walked the length of the south wall until she found the hole again. Looking around, she assessed the flexibility of the moss, vines and weeds. She held back language as the greenery fell like a broken curtain. She walked forward a few steps until she felt a familiar substance underfoot. Stone.

The air was damp and stale with a hint of wine. She looked around to see old-fashioned torches hanging on the walls and bottles in interlaced racks. She walked a few more steps before something pressed against her head once more.

'Freeze, Miss Kaisøn.'

Anonasai smiled as she raised her arms. *The fool didn't have a gun this time. No, that would be too loud and make this room a mess.* She looked right to see the wine rack just holding together, and she was close enough to grab a wine bottle and smash it behind her on the man's hand.

She watched as two wine bottles smashed, red liquid and green glass falling to the ground and creating a more significant scene. Agent Bondi held his left hand as heat and pain rippled through. He looked at Anonasai as she readied to kick him, but a noise captured her attention. Footsteps, running footsteps.

So Anonasai ran off into the dark as Noah held his hand above the mess.

'You! What did you do?' demanded an Escaian solider.

'Sorry, the bottle slipped,' lied Agent Bondi.

'We told you, these are old. Be more vigilant!'

While the men were distracted as they argued, Anonasai ran into the semi-lit hallway. The walls were of stone and smelt of damp dirt. She was in the passageway to the bunker, so she followed the hallway to an opening of a small room filled with material bags. She walked up to the bags to read the Escaian labels: flour, wheat, sugar and yeast. She looked around the room to see pots and pans hanging from a wall and an old-fashioned stove oven in a corner. A large stone island had been sculptured in the middle of the room. A low buzz soon filled the silence, making her jump. She turned quickly to the right side of the room to see a modern fridge. A shadow soon filled the room. Anonasai hid beside the stone island as someone entered the room.

A male yelled into the room before a female voice timidly replied. Footsteps scraped on the stone flooring and the room fell silent. Anonasai observed the maid walking to the fridge and she ran to the entrance. She was a step away from the door when a knife was thrown in front of her. She watched the knife bounce off the wall to her left.

Anonasai looked at the maid holding another knife in her right hand, much larger than the one thrown at her. Anonasai glared at the woman, but she put the knife down.

'Are you here to get rid of the fake Escaian?' asked the woman in a thick Escaian accent.

'You speak English.'

The woman ignored her and continued, 'If not, I'll alert the guards.'

'Yes, I'll get rid of him.'

'Good, his Escaian is horrible.'

Anonasai stared at the woman as she looked familiar in the torch light. She tried to picture her in Makino clan clothing, but couldn't. 'Do I know you?'

'No, this is first time,' replied the woman too quickly.

Anonasai grabbed a torch from the right wall, walked towards the woman, and held it close to her.

'Your hair is dyed black but the roots are brown. You have a scar on your forehead covered with make-up, and you wear this outfit to match the room, which is overkill. The shoes are straining your muscles as you walk, but you throw with intent to kill.'

'Fine, yes, I was in the Makino clan. The Head sent me here

five years ago undercover to kill a minister, but I couldn't. I fell in love with him.'

The woman revealed a scar with the letters M and C overlapping each other. The remnants of a tattoo, now damaged by jagged purple lines and the paleness of her forearm. The ink had vanished as she had removed it herself.

'What about you, miss? What are you doing?'

Anonasai showed her tattoo of the Makino clan, the M and C still black with green vines around them.

The woman paled. 'That's the upper rank tattoo.'

'Yeah.'

'I'm sorry, I …'

'Don't worry, I'm not after you.'

'Please, The Head knows I'm out.'

Anonasai rolled her eyes as she walked away from the woman. 'I don't need a story. You're safe for now. I'm hunting someone else.'

'Is it my Valentin?'

Anonasai saw the worry in her face, in her eyes. The letter did mention Valentin Silca, but as a minister in the figurehead's inner circle. Anonasai saw the woman paling more as the silence was getting to her.

'No.'

The woman breathed a sigh of relief. Anonasai looked at the supplies on the bench: flour, yeast, water and eggs. Basics for bread with a few herbs. She then looked in the fridge to see a variety of cheeses, meats and fruits. 'What is your name?'

'Sasha.'

'Your Makino name.'

'I was the AOD, Freyja.'

Anonasai looked at the woman again and smiled before asking, 'Where are your poisons?'

Sasha gestured to the stone island and Anonasai began to approach it, but Sasha stopped her.

'I want reassurance you will not hurt Valentin.'

'Oh, please.'

Sasha held Anonasai with a stern look.

'I will promise no such thing.'

'Excuse me?' As Sasha scanned the ingredients in front of her, she heard stone scraping. She looked back to see a brick removed; her secret spot was not so secret.

'*You moron*, they will hear you,' snapped Sasha in Escaian.

Anonasai looked at the brown bottles labelled in Escaian then at Sasha. She pocketed two small bottles before putting the stone back. 'Call me a moron again, and I'll slit your throat.'

'You, you understand, Escaian,' whispered Sasha.

'Yes, start cooking,' ordered Anonasai as she walked to a dark corner to conceal herself. Footsteps echoed down the corridor and Sasha headed to her station to prepare breakfast.

'Sasha, what was that noise?' asked a solider in Escaian.

'I'm cooking, can't you see?' replied Sasha. She noticed that the men at the entrance had rifles. *Something has them spooked today, and the fake Escaian man is accompanying them. Seriously, he tells the soldiers one joke, and now they are allies.*

'What was that noise?' repeated Agent Bondi in Escaian.

Sasha looked at the fake blonde Escaian then the soldiers. Agent Bondi waited for a reply. He knew he'd asked correctly. *Was she hiding something?* A soft click echoed around the room.

He identified that click; a gun is moving into position. He knew the maid had no weapons, so someone else had to be in there. Sasha breathed in deep, then glared. 'I dropped a pan, all right!' replied Sasha with attitude.

'Twice?' asked a soldier.

'Yes twice — these walls do echo,' replied Sasha as she headed over to the stone oven.

The soldiers stared at Sasha momentarily before walking away as Agent Bondi scanned the room.

As the oven heated, Sasha placed five circular pieces of dough into the oven. She turned around to see the fake Escaian behind her. She jumped, putting her right hand on her heart, her left hand knocking over brooms and metal handles. From her dark corner, Anonasai aimed her 9mm Glock at his head.

'Why are you still here? I thought you left,' grunted Sasha.

'What are you doing, Sasha?' asked Noah.

'What do you mean, sir?'

'Taking too long to answer my question, our questions … when asked in Escaian, you answer with little hesitation.'

'I do not like guns in my kitchen.'

Sasha walked to the fridge and prepared a fruit platter. Agent Bondi noticed skid marks on the ground before him.

'A pan doesn't leave skid marks on stone.'

'Detective now, are you?'

Sasha glanced over her shoulder to see him behind her again.

'They were there before I started. I don't ask questions, I just cook.'

'Don't give me that.'

Agent Bondi touched her left shoulder as a man's voice suddenly roared, 'Step away from my wife!'

Noah looked down the hallway and saw a muscular man taking up the space. He heard from the locals Valentin Silca was a tank, but to see him — he was something else.

Agent Bondi lifted his hands in surrender. The muscular man stormed to Sasha's side, staring at the man who dared touch her.

'Go before I kill you,' hissed the man in warning.

Noah retreated as the man glared at his back.

'Valentin, I had everything under control.'

'Sure, my angel. What is for breakfast?

'Why you only think of your stomach?'

'But your cooking is divine, just like you.'

Sasha blushed and walked to the stone oven holding her cheeks. 'Valentin stop it, you make me blush.' She took the golden-brown loaves out of the oven and placed the pan on the stone island before sprinkling them with herbs. Valentin grabbed one of the loaves of bread, but Sasha snatched it back.

'What?' Valentin looked at Sasha holding the loaf in her hands. From the corner of his left eye, a shadow caught his attention. He turned quickly to see a woman with a gun in hand.

Valentin stepped in front of Sasha as he put the pieces together. The woman from the shadows put her gun away and stood firm.

Valentin reached for a frying pan above the island when Sasha spoke out, 'Valentin, she's ... an upper rank from my clan.'

'Name,' demanded Valentin.

'Anonasai.'

Sasha's eyes widened at the name. The wandering assassin is in her kitchen, so she started praying to be spared from her.

'What do you want with my wife.'

Anonasai held up a brown bottle. Light from the stone oven showed the bottle was now empty. Valentin looked at the loaves of bread, then at Sasha. 'We want nothing more to do with Makino. My Sasha is out.'

'Noted.' Anonasai began walking towards the entrance.

'Wait!'

Anonasai paused. She looked behind her to see Valentin and Sasha holding hands.

'Your target, who is it?' asked Sasha.

'Makino ... don't disclose.'

Valentin pulled Sasha closer as Anonasai disappeared down the hall.

CHAPTER 9

Anonasai ran down the grey stone hallway until she found a white oak door with no hinges or handles. *So how does it open?*

She pressed a hand on the door and felt it was warm despite the bone-chilling coldness of the stone walls. Putting on her mask, she drew her Glock and pointed it down the hall as echoing footsteps rapidly approached with an odd squeaking noise. Soon, Sasha came into view pushing a wooden trolley with a white sheet draped over the top and sides.

'You shouldn't be here, Sai Sai,' whispered Sasha.

Anonasai slid her mask to the left side of her face before whispering, 'I have a target inside. We are not in the clan anymore, so don't call me Sai Sai.'

Sasha looked at Anonasai sadly as she put on her mask once more. Sasha knocked on the door three times and waited. She felt a breeze brush against her legs but she didn't react as the door slid into a cavity in the stone wall. Sasha rolled the heavy cart inside the candlelit white room with its golden archways and an extended chestnut oak table centred in the room with red carpet underneath. The table was lit with white candles in silver candleholders, and green plants with white blooming flowers were laid in the middle. *It's a beautiful centrepiece but the flowers needed a good drink of water.* Five sets of gold and white China were waiting to be filled with food as four dignitaries sat ready.

Sasha knew these people; these chosen ministers would keep her prime minister company. *One of the men was a target, so why was she doing her duty again? Why did Anonasai call upon her? True, in the Makino clan, I was the Angel of Death Freyja, and I spent a few years collecting poisons … and then there was Valentin and I stopped because of him.*

Sasha refocused as she served her herbed bread to the ministers. She stopped at an extra seat. She was cooking for five, not six. She heard the door open; she didn't look as she was instructed to never look at the prime minister as he walked in, but none of the other ministers stood. An oak chair moved beside her, and she nearly fell to the ground as Valentin sat down.

'Porridge,' Valentin demanded.

Sasha cast a worried look at her husband, but managed a nod. She made her stiffened legs walk over to her cart. *I told him everything, but why is he here? Why?*

Sasha looked over her cart and noticed that a server had taken away her cheese and fruit platter, and the damper. *Crap.* She tapped twice on the wooden cart then lifted the sheet. Anonasai was sitting beside a silver pot, her rifle in two pieces. *Where was she hiding it before?* Sasha grimaced at her friend before lifting the pot on top of the cart, filling a bowl, and taking it over to Valentin.

'Porridge, sir.'

Valentin nodded his thanks. The door opened again; the ministers and Valentin bowed. Sasha looked down as men entered. The atmosphere felt heavy as the authority figure was now in the room. She heard their footsteps walk the length of the table before a chair scraped against the carpet.

'Sit,' ordered the prime minister.

Chairs moved again, then silence. Sasha looked up to see the fake Escaian next to the prime minister, who ordered the fake Escaian to taste his food.

'I'm here to protect you, not to be your food taster.'

'It is a great privilege to be a food tester,' replied Valentin with a thick accent.

Agent Bondi looked at the foreign minister angrily then at the herb bread. He noticed that the foreign minister had a different meal than the others, but they probably knew that.

So, Noah took a knife and fork and separated the bread. He watched as a gooey substance slowly leached its way onto the plate. He cut off a section and brought it to his mouth. He smelt the aroma: a mix of herbs, bread and almonds. His gut knotted, telling him something was wrong, so he asked, 'You ... Sasha isn't it? Has anyone poisoned the prime minister before?'

'No, not while I have been here.'

Agent Bondi put the bread in his mouth before grabbing a silver goblet. 'It's fine, chewy but fine.'

The prime minister waved a hand, signalling the others to eat. Sasha grabbed the silver goblet from the fake Escaian with disgust. *How dare he insult me!* She took great pride in her cooking. Sasha looked inside the silver goblet to see the remains of food inside.

He didn't eat it! He faked it. I must warn my leader and fellow citizens of this deceit.

First, she heard thudding sounds, then clinking noises on the table. She turned around and froze as she saw the ministers' heads in their food. The prime minister's head was also in his food. *Why were they all slumped over?*

'You! what did you do?' yelled Sasha.

'Me? I did nothing,' replied Agent Bondi, confused.

Noah looked around the room to saw the door was only accessible from the inside. There were no windows, only air vents. He knew that even if the poison was airborne, he and Sasha would be dead or sleeping on the ground. Sasha ran over to Valentin and shook him. *Why did she run over to him? What was she saying?* He could only make out one word from her Escaian. *Sorry, why was she sorry?*

'Why are you sorry?' asked Agent Bondi without emotion.

Sasha glared at him as tears rolled down her face. He got it now. She was in love. 'You were his partner.'

'I am his partner,' snapped Sasha with venom.

Soldiers pounded on the door, yelling to anyone inside to let them in.

'He's dead. You're a widow,' said Agent Bondi coldly as he looked around the room.

Sasha closed her eyes and checked for Valentin's pulse. He had one; it was steady. *But why was he slumped over? Is he sleeping?*

'Face it, you're a widow now.'

Sasha opened her eyes to see the Englishman looking around the room for clues. He wasn't letting the soldiers into the bunker. Anger rose in Sasha as she looked upon the man before her. The fake Escaian, the blonde-haired, tanned man who didn't do his job, the man that suddenly turned up one day and took the place of protector. So she took a knife off the table and pointed it towards the imposter. 'How do I know you didn't poison them?'

Noah looked at the woman with the knife. Fight instincts took over as he drew his weapon. 'Don't be an idiot. Where would I get poison from?'

'You're not from here, Englishman. The storage room chemicals can be mixed into poisons.'

He narrowed his brow, then said, 'Sure, that place is a

hazard, but why would I kill the PM when I had to protect him.' He knew his reasoning wasn't getting through, so he continued, 'You're just grief-stricken … drop the knife.'

Sasha stared at him, then noticed the white sheet on her cart move.

'Did you have something to do with their deaths?'

Sasha threw the knife at the Englishman just before gunfire sounded in the bunker. She jumped at the sudden loud noise and did a mental check. Her body didn't scream in pain, the man's gun didn't flash and smoke didn't rise off the muzzle. She looked at the Englishman's body as redness started seeping through his suit's left side. The blood stain grew bigger and bigger before he fell. Sasha watched as the man hit the ground, then she saw Anonasai behind with a gun.

'Anonasai,' said Sasha with thankfulness.

'Hurry up! Soldiers will break the door soon.'

'Sai Sai, how did you do all of this?' asked Sasha.

Anonasai looked around the room for an escape route. 'I did it in front of you.'

Sasha thought back to the kitchen. First, she saw Anonasai with the brown bottle, then Noah came in, then her husband. Finally, she lifted Valentin from his chair, but she fell due to his weight.

'Little help.'

Anonasai wheeled the cart over and lifted Valentin onto

the lower part of the cart. Sasha pushed it to the far left-hand side of the room.

'This way.'

Sasha felt along the wall until she found a loose brick and pushed it. The white brick moved aside, revealing a dark tunnel. But first, they had to get down the stairs.

'Help me with the cart,' ordered Sasha.

Anonasai pulled Sasha back from the entrance then kicked the cart down the stairs. Sasha watched in shock as the cart flew down, smashing into pieces on the landing. Anonasai grabbed her stunned ally, pulling her inside. The tunnel door sealed shut behind them.

Sasha lit a torch on the stone wall then ran to Valentin. He was still in one piece.

'What did you do to my husband? You assured me he wouldn't get hurt!' snapped Sasha.

'I did, but I couldn't guarantee you wouldn't hurt him.'

Anonasai towered over Sasha and most likely had an advantage in this space, but she knew this tunnel. She faced Anonasai. 'What did you use? When did you use it?'

'I put cyanide in your bread mixture.'

Sasha's eyes widened and she clenched her fists.

Anonasai added, 'And I put diazepam in the oatmeal.'

'Diazepam?!' Sasha looked at her husband once more. 'That would explain his heartbeat, but was it necessary to kick him down the stairs? You could've killed him.'

Anonasai scoffed and grabbed the torch off Sasha. 'The amount I used wouldn't kill a mouse.

Sasha rechecked her husband, then looked at Anonasai as the light dimmed. 'I meant when you kicked him down the stairs, and you know I can't carry him.'

Anonasai looked back at her ally and her sleeping husband; he would wake in a few hours. No doubt this facility was on high alert now; no doubt Sasha would become helpful later. So, she walked back and gave Sasha the torch before lifting her heavy husband. 'Hurry up and lead the way.

Sasha nodded and ran down the tunnel for three minutes before turning left then right. Anonasai groaned a few times as she followed Sasha through the tunnel, which ascended before landing on another set of stairs.

The entrance was dirtier than the one they had entered. Cobwebs lined the top corners and lodged on Valentin's head. Dirt had built up on the ground, but the smell wasn't that of dust, it was more of chemicals and coffee. Sasha pulled a lever then watched as more torchlight entered the tunnel. She heaved herself into the room to see bottles of chemicals and coffee beans. However, the light was not from torches but from lighting from the modern era. 'We can rest here,' she said.

'You have modern technology down here?' asked Anonasai.

'Yes. Builders dug down and set this room up.'

Anonasai took a bottle of alcohol, salt and something else, and put them into a bowl while Sasha propped up Valentin against a wall. Sasha put the bowl under his nose and watched as her husband came around.

'Sasha?'

'I'm here, my husband.'

'What happened?'

'I'm so sorry. I didn't know.'

Valentin rubbed his head and looked at his suit covered in splinters, dirt and cobwebs. He saw Sasha with the high-ranking woman. *What was her name again? Anon, Sai … Oh right, Anonasai.*

'Why are you still here? Why does my head hurt?' he asked Anonasai.

Anonasai was too busy looking out of the doorway to answer him. Too busy looking up and down, listening to Escaian as it echoed down the stone hallway.

'Valentin, it's horrible. They are dead, all are dead,' moaned Sasha.

'Who are?' Valentin looked at Sasha and saw so much sorrow.

Suddenly, everything returned to his memory — the other ministers in the room had steaming bread on their plates. Then the prime minister walked in with the Englishman. The prime minister gave them the signal to eat, so they all ate.

Valentin quickly rose to his feet despite his aching head. 'What did she do?!' asked Valentin angrily.

'She put cyanide in the bread and diazepam in your porridge,' replied Sasha timidly.

Valentin looked at Sasha for a few seconds as he felt his face turn red due to his blood pressure rising. He faced Anonasai, 'You cur, I told you my Sasha was out.'

Valentin stumbled angrily towards Anonasai, but she said, 'The fake Escaian lies dead with a hole in the heart and the bullet is untraceable to you or Sasha.'

Valentin stood silently but he was too angry to understand what the assassin had said. He repeated the information in his head, which wasn't reassuring, so he asked, 'How can I trust what you say?'

'You're alive, are you not?'

Valentin was awake, alive, and still with his love, but he was unsure of Anonasai's voice. *It sounds horrible and eerie in this stone room. Was it her mask?*

Anonasai turned to look at Valentin, and this time he saw her mask, and he jumped with fear. Sasha's was all white, and Anonasai's nearly scared him to death in the dark of night, for the assassin's mask was more horrifying and creepier. The black cracks drew him in; however, the heart soothed him. He couldn't take in the other details as her white eyes were soulless. Anonasai looked behind him to Sasha before looking back down the hallway.

'Valentin, we are traitors to your country, we must leave,' said Sasha, grabbing Valentin's right arm and pulling him away.

Anonasai faced them both. 'We will go to my brother's

land. He will take us in.'

'I don't trust your brother,' disclosed Sasha, crossing her arms.

'I know, my love, but he is all we have right now,' reassured Valentin.

'Be quiet. We must leave now before …' hissed Anonasai.

Sirens started to blare. Anonasai looked at the red light in the storage room. It rotated once, twice, three times before she walked over and disabled it with the bottom of her Glock. The room turned white once more until a woman in a suit entered.

CHAPTER 10

Valentin stood in front of Sasha as Anonasai faced the woman wearing a suit and high-tech glasses. She had tan skin, and her afro had been straightened and tied into a tight ponytail.

'Who are you?' questioned Valentin.

'You're Valentin Silca, Foreign Minister of Escya, and the woman behind you is Sasha Silca,' announced the woman in the suit.

Sasha looked at her friend with a gun. She couldn't speak as her gut told her the know-it-all with the glasses might have a translator.

'I see you've changed your hairstyle, Agent Rem,' declared Anonasai.

The woman stiffened a little before saying, 'I have no clue what you're talking about.'

Valentin looked between the two women; one was new to the field, and the other was a cold, heartless killer, *no doubt smiling cruelly under that mask of hers.* 'Freyja, kcuiq nur.'

Sasha tapped twice on Valentin's back as a signal, *but what of the soldiers down the hall?* Sasha gave a subtle nod and Valentin ran for the door. Remmy smiled at Anonasai, who knew something was wrong, so she fired in front of Valentin. She ensured her bullet went past Valentin to the wall in front of him as a warning. Sparks flew off the wall as she returned her attention to Rem, saying, 'You have an execution squad in the hall.'

'Rats! What gave me away?'

'No one has come down the hall since you entered, and you didn't care that Valentin and Sasha were leaving.'

Agent Rem shrugged as Valentin and Sasha walked back to the cold stone wall. Then, to prove Anonasai's theory, Sasha threw a can of beetroot into the hall and watched as it was torn violently apart by silent gunfire. Sasha looked at what remained: wine-coloured juice sprayed the four walls as uneven chunks of beetroot and tin lay on the stained stone floor. She glared at the woman as that could've been Valentin and herself, but her hatred soon went as Sai Sai saved them.

Valentin looked at the woman he thought was new to the killing field. Instead, she was a pro, a mistake he wouldn't make again.

'The wandering assassin, by order of the king, you are under arrest.'

Three men in black filled the doorway with military-grade auto-weapons.

'Which king do you speak of?' retorted Anonasai.

'I shall not speak his name. You will see for yourself.'

Anonasai moved her head slightly down as the atmosphere filled with murderous intent. Sasha opened the tunnel door behind her and she and Valentin escaped. There were three rounds of gunfire before silence filled the space.

'Sasha?'

'I'm okay, are you.'

'I'm okay, no holes.'

'We must prepare ourselves for the worst. Your friend could be gone,' claimed Valentin.

Sasha nodded and looked back to her husband before replying, 'Anonasai can't die. I've tried.'

'What do you mean, you've tried?'

'I tried to kill her and The Head of the Makino, but they kept getting up. No poison, no weapon, no person can kill them.' Sasha pointed to the scar on her head as she pulled a lever and waited for the stone door to open again. Three bodies were on the ground in pools of blood. Anonasai was standing in the middle of the room without a scratch. *But where was that woman, Agent Rem? Where was she?*

'Anonasai?'

Anonasai looked behind her with murderous intent. Valentin stared at the assassin and saw her white eyes slowly looking at his wife before looking at the hallway. 'She'll lead the way.'

'No, I can't do that to my friend.'

'She just killed three heavily armed men. She doesn't have a scratch on her.'

Anonasai walked over the dead and to the hallway without caution. Sasha and Valentin soon stopped their arguing. Anonasai followed the stone tunnel until she reached the wine cellar above ground. She walked a few steps, then stopped. The embassy was quiet as the alarms had stopped; the wine cellar was dark as the torches were out. Her attention was caught as the darkness started to move unevenly.

'Hide in the dark, hide low,' ordered Anonasai coldly.

Sasha pushed her husband to the left corner of the room and lay flat on the mossy ground. Seconds later, red flares came to life, lighting up the room. She could see five men in green and gold uniforms — the prime minister's elite guards. Anonasai stepped closer to a wine rack, but Valentin ran into view. He spoke to the guards. Finally, the elite guards stepped aside so Valentin and the masked woman could leave. They reached the archway and waited for Sasha, but she was waiting for them.

'Wait,' said Anonasai. She had a wine bottle with dry material stuffed into it.

'Anonasai, no, they let us go. We need to leave,' pleaded Sasha.

'She doesn't have the guts to do that. Besides, wine isn't flammable,' reassured Valentin.

Anonasai shrugged then dropped the glass bottle onto the ground. Sasha and Valentin looked at the broken remnants of the brown glass and the white material and black powder. They saw a faint trail, so they quickly followed it.

'Anonasai, where did you get all of that?' asked Sasha.

'Don't worry about it.'

'Where did that Agent Rem girl go?' asked Valentin.

'She ran,' replied Anonasai, disappointed.

Anonasai rounded the southeast corner of the red-brick wall, grabbed her red sports bag and put her mask inside before exiting the ground and onto the streets. Valentin fooled the police officers as he told them he was leaving the embassy with his two mistresses.

CHAPTER 11

Anonasai walked ahead of Sasha and Valentin. She was infuriated, *a mistress of all people.* As they walked down the asphalt street, all eyes turned their way. Anonasai felt she couldn't just leave them behind now. Her mission was over, however Sasha and Valentin had saved her life, and she had saved theirs, but she hated unwanted attention, so she walked back to them.

'Valentin, take off your jacket,' ordered Anonasai.

'What?' hissed Sasha.

'Pardon me?' he questioned.

'Your jacket … you stick out like a sore thumb,' declared Anonasai.

Sasha stared her friend down as Valentin looked himself over. His jacket was covered in porridge, splinters and cobwebs, *but what would you expect? I was drugged, thrown down a flight of stairs and carried through a tunnel. That's what I was told.*

'No, this jacket is the highest quality of ...'

'It's fabric with a price tag – take it off.'

Valentin stared at Anonasai's green eyes and the dried blood at her hairline. *So, she was hit in that gunfight. Sasha was right, she couldn't be killed.* He took off his jacket.

'Anonasai, thank you for saving our lives, but I have a question for you.'

'Val, no.'

'What?'

'When did you get hit in the head?'

Anonasai didn't need to touch her head to know what he was talking about. The second bullet ricocheted from the wall near her and grazed her skull. She acted like she wasn't hit, her hoodie saving her, but the soldiers didn't have a chance.

'The bullets, they were from semi-auto guns,' stated Valentin. 'No one is that quick.'

Anonasai glared at him; *he's being a pain and getting close to the truth.*

'Well, I am. This is where we part.'

Sasha nodded, holding Valentin's hand. Anonasai turned on her heels and walked down the street. Sasha and Valentin watched as she slowly vanished. As Sasha and Valentin moved again, an explosion roared behind them. They looked back at the embassy to see smoke pouring out of the east side.

Sasha thought, *The surprise that Anonasai had left on the ground was the cause no doubt, but how did it ignite? It's not our problem now. We have to flee, get off the streets where we aren't recognisable and get to Valentin's brother's land.*

CHAPTER 12

Down underground in a white marble room, along a chestnut oak table, was a crime scene with six bodies. Five bodies were hunched together on the table and one was on the red carpet in a body bag. Forensic officers took photos of the dead and placed numbers next to the deceased in the order of who died first. Samples of the food and drinks were taken off site before they readied the bodies for transport.

An officer ran back to the scene and yelled, 'Don't touch the bodies, chemicals have been identified. Special equipment is in transit. All personnel evacuate at once!'

Shortly after, the room was quiet once more. The prime minister of Escya lifted his head from his plate. He saw four bodies on the table and one black body bag. The door had been replaced with plastic sheeting that appeared to be closed off — for now.

He grabbed a napkin and wiped debris from his face. There were breadcrumbs, a gooey substance, then black and blue dots that held his false face together. He tore the tiny black dots off his face. His ears rang as his senses returned, but that didn't stop him from digging into his jacket pockets, bringing out a silver flask, and drinking. He then stared at the body bag.

Five dignitaries were at the table... no six, one had porridge. Where is he? In the bag? Then there was that spy ... maybe he poisoned us all. But why use a small body bag for a big fellow? thought the PM as he drank.

Before walking to the body bag, he washed the bitter almond taste from his mouth with the liquor. He tapped the body bag with his foot and said, 'Well, sister, you sure know how to make a mess.'

The plastic sheeting rattled, revealing a man and woman in suits entering the room. The man looked at the two new arrivals. *Bollocks, no one seems to lock doors these days.*

The dark-skinned woman drew her weapon and pointed to the fake prime minister standing next to the body bag. The man looked over to the dark-skinned male standing beside her, looking on in shock.

'Freeze!' yelled Agent Rem.

'Remmy!' whispered Agent Sharp.

'You're Rem Hitchcock,' said the fake prime minister.

'Who are you then?' yelled Remmy.

The imposter didn't reply.

'Are you in league with the wandering assassin?' asked Agent Sharp.

The imposter pocketed his flask and glared at the two agents before saying, 'You will leave Anonasai alone.'

'I take that as a yes,' said Dan.

'He's unarmed,' whispered Remmy.

'He was dead on the table. If you want to question the crazy zombie, go ahead.'

'I won't, the idiot will.'

The imposter stopped glaring as a sharp pain hit his left shoulder. His jacket had a hole and blood was seeping out. He looked at the woman to see her gun hadn't fired. The male next to her still had his weapon holstered. Then he heard the low hum of a zip unzipping.

'That was stupid. You fired blindly,' scorned the imposter.

'No, all I needed was your attention for a moment,' declared Agent Bondi as he emerged from the body bag.

The imposter saw Agent Sharp next to him with a closed fist; he moved around and dodged a blow that would've knocked him out. Instead, the imposter grabbed the agent's gun and knocked Agent Sharp unconscious.

'Now then, where were we?' asked the imposter.

'Two against one!' yelled Remmy.

'No need to state the obvious, Agent.' The imposter pointed

the 9mm Glock at Agent Bondi as he was trying to free himself from the body bag. Remmy was shaking as she realised her teammates were in danger.

'How are you alive then? I checked your pulse. You were dead,' mumbled Remmy.

The imposter chuckled. 'I was, but now I'm alive.'

'Who are you? No one can survive cyanide poisoning,' questioned Noah.

The imposter saw that Bondi was wearing a small breathing device around his neck; his white undershirt was bloody and his forehead bruised.

'Constantine Knight,' revealed the imposter.

Remmy paled as her glasses fed her no information. 'You're lying. Your name doesn't exist.'

Constantine knew that the glasses she was wearing were the same that Truth wore. He rolled his eyes; modern technology had its flaws. So, he pulled apart the 9mm Glock and dropped it in front of Agent Bondi before walking towards Remmy.

'Freeze!' yelled Agent Bondi.

Constantine continued to walk, so Noah fired. Constantine caught the bullet in his right hand and took Remmy's glasses off her. He put them. He saw nothing. Remmy looked at him, confused. Constantine scanned the bullet he caught to see an information overload. The batch number, the gun model, ownership blackened, DNA unknown.

'Where are you from?' demanded Rem.

No reply.

'It's okay. You can trust me.'

'Rem Hitchcock, you work with South Row PD, MI5 and MI6. You specialise in technology and leave no trace but leave a mess with vehicle footprints.'

'It's called a ... vehicle footprint.'

'You've gone through thirty cars in five years.'

'Blame those two field agents, not me.'

Constantine lifted an eyebrow. *Surely, she wasn't serious. The dark one, yes, but the wanna-be, no.*

'Remmy, move!' ordered Agent Bondi.

'I can make that body bag of yours permanent for you, Agent,' Constantine threatened.

Noah looked down at the bag then back at Remmy and Constantine. He had no weapon, and he couldn't possibly flick a bullet. However, he wasn't in the mood to get shot twice, so Agent Bondi lowered his gun.

'So, where are you from? You didn't answer me.'

No reply.

'It's okay,' reassured Rem.

'Great London,' revealed Constantine.

'That doesn't exist,' said Bondi.

'Wait, wait ... what year was it in Great London?'

'1666.'

Information flooded the glasses of 1666, so Constantine

took them off.

Rem looked sadly at Constantine, thinking he looked so young and had probably done many horrible things. 'Why doesn't your name exist?' whispered Rem.

Constantine hated killing people – he decided that his sister could clean up this loose end. *But no, these three must have family who love them. I have a family that loves me.* 'Ask Anna.' Constantine opened the plastic sheeting then walked out.

'Well, that's rude,' said Remmy.

'Who cares? Let's go,' replied Bondi, pulling up Agent Sharp.

'Do you think he has a sister?' asked Remmy

'Yes, he said ask Anna.'

'Maybe her name is an alias. Perhaps ... Anna Knight'

Remmy stopped and searched all the information flooding her glasses. She saw a family tree, a map of Great London, an old family photo, then nothing. Remmy returned to the family tree to see Anna's name and Constantine's. A line underneath was censored. A child.

CHAPTER 13

Anonasai entered the Escaian airport but no planes were taking off. News had already spread that the prime minister of Escya had been killed, but no more information had been relayed and hundreds of citizens were in an uproar. She recognised familiar faces and walked over to Sasha, Valentin and Hyosuke as they sat in a corner.

'What are you doing?' asked Anonasai.

'Fleeing the country, but the acting government has given a no-fly order,' replied Sasha.

Hyosuke looked at Anonasai, then asked her, 'What did you do?'

The white noise of people's conversations and wrath soon grew thunderous. Anonasai pointed to the television over her shoulder. Hyosuke couldn't understand Escaian, but he read the English words, *Rest in Peace*.

'Hunting Bird, did you complete your mission?'

Anonasai nodded. Hyosuke closed his eyes then breathed out a long sigh. *This was why no planes were flying out, and why everyone's grounded.*

Anonasai sat next to Hyosuke and whispered, 'Remember, Freyja. This is her.'

'Sorry, who are you?' Valentin asked Hyosuke.

'Kotoshi Hyosuke, allies with Anonasai.'

'Good, we are all friends then,' replied Sasha.

'Are you Makino?' asked Hyosuke.

'Was …' replied Sasha and Valentin in unison.

'Sasha was Freyja in the Makino. Her last mission was to kill Valentin Silca. Unfortunately, she didn't complete it,' explained Anonasai.

'Why not?' asks Hyosuke.

Sasha blushed. 'I fell in love.'

Hyosuke smiled then turned to face Anonasai, who looked out the window. 'Anonasai, what is it?'

'I must get to the Escaian and Republic of Telfax border.'

'That's suicide!' hissed Hyosuke.

'Why?' asked Sasha.

'Last part of my mission. How far away is it?'

'About five hundred miles, give or take. It's still suicide,' said Valentin.

Hyosuke spoke softly, 'Hunting Bird, why is it important that you must go there?'

'Hunting Bird?' queried Sasha.

Anonasai leaned close to Hyosuke and whispered, 'The Mace of House.' She then kissed Hyosuke's cheek and headed for the exit.

'What's a hunting bird, Hyosuke?' asked Sasha.

'It's my name for her.'

'But she is an assassin,' murmured Valentin.

'When she has to be,' Hyosuke added, as he wistfully watched Anonasai disappear into the crowd. He hated when she disappeared as he didn't know when she would return. So, he turned his attention back to Sasha and her husband, whose name he didn't yet know. Sasha looked worried and her husband was already standing. Hyosuke wondered why he was so defensive … that's when he saw a ghost from the past.

CHAPTER 14

Anonasai walked around the streets until she found a quiet space. She took out her phone and headset then rang Ping. The line rang three times. An automatic voice answered before another voice came through.

'Anonasai?' whispered Ping.

'Ping, why are you whispering?'

'No reason,' replied Ping defensively.

'Are you at the Makino clan's mansion?'

'No.'

'Is The Head around?'

'No.'

'Are members around?'

'No.'

Anonasai started to panic. Ping had never left the mansion before. She searched her surroundings and saw citizens in their own world. Cars that wouldn't be of any use to her. Then she thought back to the hotel. She listened to Ping's background and heard a whining noise. It was a faint whine, but it was an engine.

'Are you on a bloody plane?' asked Anonasai.

'Yes, it's cold up here.'

'The cargo hold will be pressurised at least. The temperature is usually between seven and eighteen degrees depending on its cargo. Ping, what the hell were you thinking? How high up are you?'

'Thirty thousand feet.'

Anonasai heard a roar of an engine and saw the latest green Mercedes Benz AMG GT R. The driver had just walked away, so she walked up to the vehicle, broke the driver's side window, pressed the start engine, got in and took off.

'Keep talking to me, Ping.'

'About what?'

'Anything. No limits.'

'I have the Mace of House.'

'Is that why you're on that plane?'

'Yes, Oxy wasn't picking up. You killed Sax, and Hermes is on another job.'

'What job? I didn't assign him to any jobs.'

'The Head sent Hermes to find Oxy. Unfortunately, some police officer captured her.'

Anonasai drove from the inner city to the outer lands where she broke the speed limit.

'Do you have a parachute?'

'Yes, why?'

'How far are you from the drop point?'

'A few miles.'

Anonasai looked at the navigation system in the Mercedes. She was miles away.

'How did you become immortal?'

Anonasai sighed. She did say no limits. 'I was in a fire that consumed my hometown. There was smoke. My brother took us away from the fire and smoke until a black cloud engulfed us. We breathed in the black cloud, and we've been immortal ever since then.'

There was silence on the phone

'Ping ... Ping, answer me!' yelled Anonasai with urgency.

'Sorry, I'm just tired.'

'Don't fall asleep. Tell me how we first met.'

'Okay, I was fifteen, it was Halloween night, and my friends came to the villa in the hills. We broke in, and they trashed the home. I went into the garage and hacked a vintage model Honda NSX. The garage door opened, and you were standing there with your mask. I tried to run you over, but you disabled the vehicle. My friends ran off, leaving me behind.' Ping laughed. 'You tore off the car door to get me out, then stopped. Then came the choice you gave to your followers.'

'Ping, stay on track.'

'You gave me a choice. Die at fifteen or follow you.'

'Put your mask on, Ping.'

'Okay, why?'

A few moments later, Anonasai heard a loud buzz on the phone. Ping started to freefall from the plane. Anonasai heard her screaming. She drove faster to a no-drive zone. Seeing barricades before her, she drove through them as she spotted a white parachute in the distance. The line went dead and Anonasai ripped the headset from her ear, making it bleed. She put the hazard lights on and blared the horn before coming to a stop. A soldier ran up to her as she left the vehicle, yelling at her to stop. She shoots him and doesn't watch as the body fell in a heap. She kept an eye on the parachute descending.

Her eyes turned white as she ran to the rendezvous point. Within five minutes, she had run five miles and realised she had pushed herself too far as a steady stream of blood ran from her left nostril. She had a dull headache but ignored the pain as she wiped away her blood with her hand. The smell of copper made her feel sick but that wasn't important as she frantically searched the field of dirt. Here she saw a familiar view of large craters, unexploded missiles, and barricades. Some barricades had holes blasted in them, some had fire damage, and some were torn down. Anonasai desperately looked around until she saw a white parachute caught on barricades. She began to run towards the parachute when a voice yelled behind her. She froze, put on her mask and drew her weapon.

She turned around with a gun in hand to see a soldier in camouflage with two blue bands on his arms. She put her weapon away and approached the man. 'There is nothing out there, foreigner.'

Those weren't the right words. 'Your boss didn't tell you who you were meeting, did he?'

'Right. Freedom to the Republic of Telfax, for freedom and glory.'

'Smile to the enemy, it may not kill them, but it kills their egos.'

The soldier recognised the coded message and nodded his approval before leading her to a small concrete box. Inside was a woman in black, her head down, wearing a grey backpack.

'I found her on the battlefield. I thought her dead when she fell from the sky.'

Anonasai tried the door handle but it jammed on her.

'I have the key,' offered the soldier.

'I have my key,' replied Anonasai as she punched the glass.

She opened the door with so much force that the solider looked twice and was surprised to see it was still attached. He knew she didn't care about the door as she walked straight to the young woman sitting in the little concrete box. Anonasai took off the young woman's mask and saw her ghostly white skin.

Ping was breathing. She checked her pulse. It was unsteady. The young woman's lips were blue, however they were starting to redden. *The box was warm but was it warm enough?* Anonasai looked at Ping's hair. She hadn't dyed her fiery red hair or changed her mask. *So, she was still in the Makino clan.*

'Ping.'

'Hmm?' replied Ping quietly.

'You know her?' asked the solider.

'Yes, she's a … friend.'

Ping opened her emerald-green eyes and recognised Anonasai in front of her.

'Ping.'

'Hi.'

'How long has she been in and out of consciousness?' Anonasai asked the soldier.

'Ever since I found her. She said to wait for you.'

Anonasai stood and opened Ping's backpack and found a first aid kit and the Mace of House in three pieces. Anonasai got three heat packs out, cracked them and placed them in Ping's jacket. Anonasai then put the golden pieces together before handing the Mace of House to the solider.

Ping grabbed the mace from the soldier and glared at him, saying, 'How can we trust you?'

'Telfaxian soldiers have one blue band on their arms. Soldiers that serve the prime minister have two or more, depends on their inner circle.'

Ping looked at Anonasai then the soldier before releasing her hold on the mace. The soldier bowed and left. Anonasai helped Ping as they walked back to the Mercedes. Ping threw the heat packs to the side of the road and Anonasai took off.

'Where are we going?' asked Ping.

'We're to pick up Freyja.'

'Freyja is here? But she's been missing for so long.'

Anonasai rounded a bend before slamming on the brakes. She turned the wheel to make the Mercedes drift to a stop. She death-stared the figure in cream clothing and mint-coloured vest wearing a white mask. She could've driven around him but her instincts made her stop. *Am I actually seeing him? Is he really in front of me?*

'Why is The Head here?' questioned Ping.

Anonasai breathed in deeply before exiting the car. She walked in front of The Head and crossed her arms.

'What do you want, brother?'

CHAPTER 15

Anonasai stared at her brother, waiting for a reply. He was taking too long and she loathed waiting. She heard a deafening roar of an engine before seeing a 1943 GMC Army truck, the green exterior replaced with camouflaged paint. The two-seater cabin extended to a fit six personnel. Unfortunately, the windscreen was too dark to see the driver. Ping held up Anonasai's gun and aimed at The Head.

'Put that down, Ping! That will hurt you more than anyone else here,' yelled The Head.

'Do not yell at her,' snapped Anonasai.

'I've told you before to have your weapons under lock and key, sister.'

'I'm wearing a jacket, besides, it's a tranquilliser, not one that goes boom,' explained Ping.

'Anonasai, you gave a child a tranquilliser? … Our child.'

'Of course not. Ping gets stolen goods from Hermes and you. Ping is my daughter, not yours.'

'Ouch. The truck is a peace othering. You can come with me or you can find your own way off this country,' offered The Head.

Anonasai looked back at Ping then at the truck. 'Who's inside?'

'Freyja, her husband, and that man who broke into my clan.'

Oh, how I wanted to shoot my brother. His words were kind at first but he always had disdain and hatred for Hyosuke. She only had to signal Ping and she would shoot through the glass. However, she knew the glass would mess up with the trajectory or he would dodge it. So, Anonasai held her right arm to her side and with her right hand, she signalled Ping. Ping took out her phone and dialled a number. A male voice answered. His voice was thick with an accent and full of wisdom. 'Hello?'

'Where are you?'

'Where? I'm in a truck.'

'Is Freyja with you?'

'Yes, Ping … trust Anonasai,' reassured the male voice.

Ping hung up and exited the Mercedes to Anonasai's side. She handed over Anonasai's tranquilliser to her before they headed towards the truck. Anonasai opened the back passenger door where Freyja and Hyosuke sat. *My brother was honest, for once.* Ping smiled and climbed in, but Anonasai pulled her back.

'Do you have a plan to leave Escya, Constantine?' asked Anonasai.

'Yes, we go to the Escaian border and cross.'

'Ping, honey, come in. This could get ugly,' said Sasha.

Ping looked at Freyja, Hyosuke and Valentin, then Anonasai, before climbing into the truck.

Anonasai took a deep breath and asked Constantine, 'Which border are you referring to?'

'We're heading to Belarus.'

Anonasai walked past her brother with a side glare, opened the Mercedes' back passenger door, grabbed her sports bag, and returned to the truck.

'Do you have a plan when the border soldiers ask us for passports?'

Constantine walked to the back of the truck and opened the dark green curtains. Anonasai noticed that the army truck had the same old green seats and reinforced steel replaced the old wooden flooring. She climbed inside and inspected the back, bumping her forehead on something hard.

'It's a false back, enough room for Freyja, Ping and that officer to hide,' informed Constantine.

'And me.'

'Excuse me?'

'Your plans always do have flaws.'

Constantine muttered to himself before crossing his arms and saying, 'If you must.'

He walked to the front of the truck to ride shotgun. Anonasai joined Freya, Ping and Hyosuke in the back as a twelve-hour drive began.

'You're leaving the Mercedes behind?' queried Sasha.

'Yes.'

'Aren't you worried about being traced?' enquired Valentin.

'No.'

Hyosuke chuckled as Anonasai clicked her fingers. On cue, the Mercedes blew up into a fireball.

'I liked that car,' said Ping.

'Of course you did, you have her taste,' scoffed The Head with little interest.

'Ya ub'yu tebya,' said Valentin in Escaian.

'Valentin …' hissed Sasha in warning.

'No one can kill me. Many have tried, and many have failed,' disclosed The Head.

Sasha looks at Anonasai and mouthed, 'He knows Escaian.'

'And one hundred and ninety-four other languages.'

Sasha sighed in defeat. 'It's going to be a long twelve hours.'

'Head, what's the plan on dogs?' enquired Ping.

'Dogs?'

'All border forces have different searching techniques. Many have soldiers, technology and dogs.'

Constantine looked at Ping. She had a point. The

reinforced steel and lead will disrupt the technology of this age, so soldiers will have to do a visual check … but dogs.

'Where is the nearest orchard?' asked The Head.

'Three hours away … why?' answered Valentin.

'Well, take us there,' demanded The Head.

'Why the orchard?' asked Hyosuke.

'Dogs dislike the smell of citrus, along with alcohol, vinegar and certain perfumes,' said Anonasai.

There is silence as Valentin continued driving towards the nearest orchard. When they arrived, most of the fruit was still green. They were too far away from town to gather other supplies. But Anonasai had an idea. 'Wait till nightfall.' She pointed to a lime orchard over the road.

Constantine smiled, 'Thieves of Nyx.'

'Thieves of Nyx,' repeated Anonasai.

'Nyx, who is Nyx?' asked Hyosuke.

'It's a clan thing,' replied Ping.

Anonasai and The Head walked over to the orchard and looked around.

'Anonasai is no longer a clan member, so why is she helping that man?' questioned Valentin.

Ping replied, 'Anonasai is in the clan. She just works on the outside.'

'So, she is a rogue. I like her better now,' said Valentin with a smile.

'Of course you do, honey.' Sasha placed a hand on her

husband's shoulder before continuing, 'Valentin, remember when I said she is an upper rank.'

'So she takes orders from the man in white, the one you call The Head.'

'Yes, honey, but Anonasai always works alone.'

'Sometimes,' said Hyosuke.

Anonasai and The Head split up to find a way in when darkness took over while Ping, Hyosuke, Sasha and Valentin stayed with the truck.

'So, wait until nightfall, then what?' asked Valentin.

'Go to Belarus,' replied Hyosuke.

'I have no passport,' revealed Sasha.

'Mine's in the truck,' said Hyosuke.

'I don't need one,' added Ping.

Sasha looked at Ping with a small smile.

'You need a passport to go to different lands,' explained Hyosuke.

'I know, but I don't need one. I made an internal chip that can be scanned at any airport or checkpoint.' She pressed on her wrist, 'Ta-dah … Ping.'

Sasha, Hyosuke and Valentin looked at the blue light emitting from Ping's wrist. The light shone onto the truck and showed her picture, name, birthday and unknown address.

'Ping, do your parents know about this?' enquired Valentin.

Hyosuke tightened his jaw at this question, which Sasha noticed.

'Know what?'

'That you have that.' Valentin pointed to the implant.

'No, I made it myself. It still has a few glitches, but ...'

'How did you make it?' asked Sasha.

Ping looked at Sasha with excitement, but then she remembered the clan rules. Sasha saw the excitement disappear quickly. Anonasai and The Head were seen walking back.

'Don't worry,' whispered Sasha.

'There are three ways into the orchard, but there are cameras,' disclosed The Head.

'Why have cameras on an orchard?' asked Sasha.

'Thieves,' replied Valentin.

'Funny ... Ping, can you hack in and give us fifteen minutes to collect the fruit?'

Ping looked at Anonasai. Sure she could do it, but there was one problem. 'I don't have my gear, and that's a short window.'

'It's all the time we need.' Anonasai handed over her phone.

Ping pressed a few buttons, looked at the building, then returned her attention to the phone.

'Okay, I'm in, but there isn't any security system, only a watering system.'

'Excellent!' responded The Head with delight.

Anonasai backhanded The Head's head. 'It's too easy.'

'Oh come on, in and out without a problem — a piece of cake.'

Nightfall came, lights came on, and the winter chill sent Sasha, Valentin and Hyosuke into the warmth of the truck as silence fell. The Head and Anonasai put on their masks then started stretching.

'Best of luck, sister.'

'Thieves don't believe in luck, remember, brother?'

Constantine looked at his sister with white eyes. 'So cold.'

Anonasai and The Head finished their stretching and stood behind the truck staring at the targeted orchard.

Anonasai squinted. 'Ping?'

'Right … three, two, one, go!'

The two siblings took off without a sound, only the wind disturbing the earth under their feet.

CHAPTER 16

Ping stood beside the truck in the bone-chilling night air. She felt nothing as she looked into the darkness. Sasha relaxed back into the leather sets. 'Hyosuke, what happened between you and The Head?

'Why do you ask?'

'Since he took us from the airport, The Head hasn't addressed you by your proper name. Plus, the atmosphere is tense and you're nervous. But with Anonasai, you are more relaxed.'

'I had a team, a taskforce before retirement. My team and I infiltrated the Makino clan's home. We stormed the place and took everyone into custody. That's when she walked into the room. My men attacked her. One by one, they went down, and she stood there with cracks in that mask. She left me alone to explain.'

'How many were on your team?' asked Valentin.

'Ten.'

'Did she kill them?' asked Sasha.

'No, Anonasai stopped her violence and allowed me to explain why my team and I were there. As I explained, she amended her mask. That was the first time I saw her face.'

Sasha looked out the window to see Ping still looking into the darkness.

'Are you that child's father?' asked Valentin.

'Yes.'

Sasha looked at Valentin and shook her head. But Valentin wouldn't be silenced. 'Do tell.'

'Valentin!' hissed Sasha.

'It's not so romantic,' said Hyosuke.

'Neither is our story,' revealed Valentin.

Hyosuke gave Sasha and Valentin a curious look.

CHAPTER 17

Sasha looked through the truck's window as the darkness started to blend with her memories. They were blurred at first then cleared … she exited the plane's hold … the blues and white mixed until she picked up a brown leather bag. The Angel of Death took her leather bag of poisons from Customs that they quickly searched. She had to give them some credit. Her beauty was breath-taking, and the poor men were practically falling over themselves. She was this era's Helen of Troy, and it flattered her ego until she entered the streets and everyone ignored her. That was until a black van escort sped to the sidewalk. Two men in teal uniforms jumped out and grabbed her off the street. They threw her in the back with her leather bag. She checked her poisons. However, a solider soon took her bag away from her.

'Do be careful with that — it's expensive medicine.'

'Sure, madam.'

A soldier opened the leather bag and pulled out a paper slip which he read and showed his comrade.

'Freyja. What is Freyja?'

'Freyja is my name.'

The men looked at the woman in black attire with brown hair and blue eyes. She didn't look like a doctor, too pretty, too young, and they couldn't read the labels on the bottles in her bag.

'Why you here?' enquired a soldier with an Escaian accent.

Freyja looked at the man as she thought the question over. She couldn't tell him the truth — 'I'm here to kill the foreign minister of this land.' Instead, 'A minister is ill, and I'm here to treat him.'

The men looked at each other. They knew they had to pick up a young brunette from the airport, but they knew nothing of a minister being sick.

They looked at the woman's papers again. Not that they would make sense a second time. It was in a language they couldn't read, and she didn't show signs of nervousness; she sat there staring at them.

'If you don't mind, I'd like my belongings back,' said Freyja, holding out a hand.

The men looked at her. They quickly returned her bag and papers as the journey stopped. The van doors opened; the men quickly exited the van and from view. Freyja didn't wait for instructions as she walked into the white building with golden domes. She walked through the shaded oak doors and came to a crossroad. *Do I take the left or the right hallway?* A maid walked towards her with a silver tray with towels rolled up. She said something in Escaian that Freyja couldn't understand.

'Follow me, Novichok,' repeated the maid in English.

Freyja followed the maid down white hallways, through more oak doors and into an indoor sauna. There were thirty men of different ages and shapes in pools of hot liquid and she hoped they were clothed. She followed the maid to another room, where she placed the rolled towels in an alcove.

'Why are you here, Novichok?'

Freyja looked at the woman with black hair tied back; she wore a teal uniform with a white apron.

'I'm here to treat a patient.'

The maid finished restocking towels when Freyja heard a metallic sound. The maid turned and faced Freyja.

'No one here is sick.' said the maid.

'That isn't what was reported. I will leave once I see my patient.'

'Why would we send for a foreigner when we have better doctors.'

Freyja scowled at the women as she knew she had something against her. Then Freyja realised that the maid wasn't just restocking towels.

'Are you done with the towels and the knife you have?' asked Freyja

The woman stiffened and paled. 'Knife, what knife?'

'The knife you scraped on the shelf while restocking.'

The woman revealed a small dagger and swung at Freyja, who backed into the door but dodged the blade.

'Ty mozhesh' uvernut'sya, noh ya ves yeshche tebya.'

'Speak English!' snapped Freyja in frustration as she dodged.

The maid stared intensely at Freyja as her leather bag fell to the ground. Freyja felt a slight sting on her left shoulder then she understood what was said. She pulled off a red hairband from her wrist and tied her hair back. 'Don't want to mess up my hair.'

The maid nodded in agreement. Little did she know, Freyja was getting serious.

'What's your name?' asked Freyja dodging another attack

'We don't have formalities,' replied the maid, lunging again.

Freyja caught the maid mid-swing and used her weight and momentum against her, throwing her into the door. Freyja watched as the door burst open from the impact, the hinges still attached to the wall with nails exposed. She heard water splashing with force as male occupants fled. Freyja walked out of the door to see no sign of the female she was fighting. There was blood on the cream tiled floor.

Suddenly, something caught her eye but was too late to

dodge the blade that cut her chest. It wasn't deep, just a flesh wound. If she wanted to end this quicker than a fist fight, her poisons would do, but there would be collateral damage if it got in the water, and The Head would not be pleased.

Freyja looked around the room quickly to see three stacks of black rocks in the large room. Options A, B and C if fighting the killer maid went south. The sauna was now empty of all male occupants. So now she could go all out. The woman attacked again; Freyja blocked the attack before she hit the woman under the arm. The maid grunted in pain as her arm dropped limp. Freyja then stopped another stabbing attack; she disarmed the maid and slit her throat. Freyja walked away as the woman tried to save herself as blood poured from the wound. She heard the woman gurgling and coughing on her own blood before hearing a large splash.

Freyja didn't look back as she got her bag back from the towel room then made for the door. That's when she saw the woman's body face down in the blood-stained water. She was done with that little hiccup until she saw a piece of white paper peeking out of the woman's clothing. She took the piece of paper and read A.O.D. 'For me. Thanks.'

Freyja unfolded the letter and was surprised it was still dry. She stopped in the door frame. Here she saw her mission was to acquire documentation from Valentin Silca but she was interrupted when soldiers arrested her. They took her bag of poisons and dragged her to a white office with green carpet and a marble desk with floor-to-ceiling bookcases.

'Minister Valentin, my **privodym ubiytsu**.' (Minister Valentin, we have the killer).

Freyja looked at the soldier who just spoke. She didn't understand what he just said. She was used to Novichok; *whatever that meant*. Then there was the hunk of the man in the emerald chair in front of her. Minister Valentin waved the soldiers away, leaving him with a blood-stained woman.

'So, you are a killer?' asked Minister Valentin with a thick Escaian accent. *She's gorgeous. Her brown hair tied back, her blue eyes are pretty, and her black clothing tight to see her figure. A killer? We will see.*

'No sir, I defended myself from ... I'm a doctor,' she stuttered.

'A doctor?'

Minister Valentin placed a leather bag on his marble desk, her leather bag. She walked forward to his desk but he took it back. *Did he really recoil from me?* She looked into his brown eyes and eased her bag from his grasp. Looking into her bag, one of her poisons was missing.

'Looking for this?'

She looked up to see him looking at her, his stare making her feel hot. In his hand was the missing vial of handmade chloroform. Freyja smiled sweetly. 'Why yes, thank you.'

'What is it? The writing is not readable,' asked Minister

Valentin, reclining into his chair.

Now was her time to strike. 'It's perfume I got from a lovely lady.'

Valentin raised a brow before pulling off the cork and taking a whiff. He couldn't smell anything that resembled perfume. He put the cork back on as dizziness struck him hard.

'Oh, my, are you okay, sir?' asked Freyja, pretending to care.

Valentin frowned as he strained to focus on her, trying to stop the progressive dizziness, but he slumped onto his desk, making a horrible thud. The thud made her jump, but that was the first sign it worked. She pried her vial from his grip and cried for help.

Guards raced into the room and assisted the minister. They yelled orders at each other in Escaian, but during the panic, Freyja calmly said, 'He needs to sleep off his exhaustion, the poor man. See that paperwork there? So much for one man.'

The guards looked at the pile of paper on the minister's desk. A guard looked at her and shrugged; *she was a doctor; she knew best.* So, they radioed for two strong men to aid the minister to a vehicle, and someone would drive him home. Freyja quickly gathered the foreign minister's belongings and followed the soldiers as they left the Escaian Embassy. The driver drove three hours from the city to the countryside. There she saw all sorts of beautiful views before woodland blocked her view.

'Posti pam,' said the driver.

'I don't speak Escaian!' hissed Freyja.

'Nearly there,' repeated the driver.

Freyja looked through the front windscreen and saw a beautiful cottage-like house on the hill surrounded by hedges, but the view was soon spoiled as men in camouflage uniforms approached the vehicle.

The driver spoke to the soldiers as they did their visual check on the vehicle before letting it pass. She wished she'd taken a course in Escaian from Anonasai or The Head, as she understood nothing. However, the driver soon aided her in getting the foreign minister inside and onto his bed before disappearing.

With Foreign Minister Valentin sleeping, she looked around his home for documents to make the Escaian government fall or at least someone fall. She started in the back study, tearing files apart. She grew frustrated as she understood nothing, so she took a break. She walked to the minister's room to ensure he was still sleeping.

She walked close to his bed and sat next to him. She stared at his delicate features. She then looked at his muscular body and imagined herself being held in those arms — the warmth, the security of a strong man at her side. Just thinking about it made her feel happy.

Then there was her line of work. She was Freyja, Angel of Death, killer with poisons, and … She looked at the minister again to see his eyes twitching, so she reached into her leather bag and brought out diazepam. She undid the dropper from the lid and dropped a single drop into his mouth.

Her break was over; now she had to find those documents.

CHAPTER 18

reyja was now in his library. In her frustration, she started throwing books and papers all over the place. *Where are those documents?* She was becoming increasingly frustrated by the minute. She looked around the room, the wine-red carpet was now covered in papers and books, the chestnut-coloured floor-to-ceiling bookcases now marked with white crosses. *Shit, leave no trace.* That was what was she was taught; it was drilled into her, but here she was in a room filled with evidence of her existence and she had a strange feeling. *Was it disappointment or have I forgotten something?* She'd reported every day with no progress; she'd kept up with her routine. Then it hit her when paper rattled behind her. The diazepam dosage was overdue. She looked over her shoulder to see him standing there.

'You, you drugged me!' Valentin stared at her and then the mess in his library 'What, what have you done?'

Freyja watched as he slowly strolled towards her. He was no threat, so she looked at the papers in her hands then said, 'You drugged yourself. You sniffed the vial.'

Valentin stopped. His mind was foggy, but he remembered her saying it was perfume.

'A good-looking woman told me it was perfume.'

'Well, she lied to you … good-looking!' Freyja threw papers at the minister. 'I'm beautiful, you big oaf!' yelled Freyja angrily.

He smiled wryly. He liked brunettes with fire, and this brunette was fierier than the last one he dated.

'You are trashing my library. Why?'

'I'm looking for documents for my boss,' Freyja said boldly.

'What does he want?'

'He wants …' Freyja looked at the minister, who was staring at her intently. 'How do you know my boss is male?'

'Your tone of voice. You have little interest when you talk about him.'

Freyja didn't move, not even an inch as he moved closer and closer to her. She stared into his eyes long enough to see the foggy look disappear from them. She reacted too late as he clasped her hands into his and pushed her backwards onto a dark wooden desk. He forced her arms above her head.

'I should kill you for drugging me for a week and looking at my files!' snapped Valentin with anger.

Freyja looked into his eyes to see he was trying to look mad. He reached for his pocket but she couldn't see what was there. Dread filled her as she feared the unknown, so she closed her eyes, took a risk, and kissed him.

Valentin froze as her soft lips touched his. She'd stopped, but he soon kissed her back, then he recoiled to ask, 'You don't have poison on your lips, do you?'

Freyja looked Valentin in the eyes before saying, 'No.'

He gazed into her blue eyes again and felt satisfied with her answer. He kissed her again and released her arms. She wrapped her arms around his neck as he placed his hand on her hips.

'Why don't we take this to the bedroom,' said Freyja seductively.

Valentin lifted her up, carried her to his room, and closed the door.

CHAPTER 19

As the truck rocked forward and back, Sasha was soon brought back to reality. She looked towards Ping once again to see the happiness on her face. Anonasai and her brother had returned from the orchard. The left passenger door opened, letting the chill into the truck's cabin. Ping and Anonasai quickly climbed in without a sound. The winter's chill soon entered again as The Head climbed into the front passenger seat, his clothes covered with green sap and blood stains. Valentin started the engine without a command and drove towards the Belarusian border.

'What happened to him?' asked Sasha with concern.

'No cameras, but there were traps.'

'Shut up, sister,' hissed Constantine.

'Did you get shot?' asked Valentin with no concern.

'Barbed wire,' answered Constantine irritably.

Anonasai smiled wickedly as the truck bounced around on the bumpy off-road. Ping soon fell asleep in the hidden compartment with Sasha. Anonasai looked out the window staring at the stars as Hyosuke closed his eyes. The roar of the truck's engine soon lulled into silence as he faced past memories …

Darkness turned to dawn as Hyosuke and his stealth team ran through a forest to a black-brick mansion. They broke off in pairs to clear the perimeter. A member of the stealth team reported an open window, so they quickly regrouped at the opening and helped each other inside. Hyosuke looked around the near-empty room with little detail. One white single bed with a white desk in the right-hand corner with a black laptop. He walked over to the laptop and stuck a USB into the side. An officer slid open a door to the wardrobe and saw black female clothing.

'Close it,' ordered Hyosuke in Japanese.

The officer quickly closed the door and joined the small circle. He started to explain the plan when light engulfed the room. Hyosuke and his team promptly looked at the entrance and saw a figure in black with a white mask. An officer drew a Kahr Arms CW380 semi-auto pocket pistol with stun bullets loaded. Another member pulled a short kunai knife from his vest and threw it at the figure.

The figure in the doorway caught the kunai before rushing

in. She kicked one member in the groin, grabbed cuffs off his belt and cuffed two officers together before kicking over the one with the semi-auto pistol. Another member of the stealth team grabbed his baton, straightened it and hit her left leg. Her eyes turned white as she kicked the man in the stomach, sending him to the open window. Hyosuke caught the man and watched the woman as she struck the eighth member of the stealth team to the ground.

Was she toying with them? She had a weapon in her hand, and it wasn't bleeding. Hyosuke's concern was heightened when the officer beside him started to cough up blood into his hand before collapsing to the ground. So Hyosuke drew his black dragon and yelled at the figure to freeze.

The figure soon stopped her assault.

He could see the kunai in her hand but now he saw the blood on it. He looked at his fellow officers. He saw minor injuries; however, the officer next to him who coughed up blood had severe injuries.

Hyosuke looked at her mask and saw cracks under her left eye. It wasn't damaged before the fight; something hit it or someone on his team. Then there were her eyes, all white with black irises. While she stared at him, she didn't fight back as an officer subdued her and brought her down to her knees; the knife was removed, revealing a laceration on her right palm.

Hyosuke told his team to calm down while they held her

down. He took off her white cracked mask and held it in his hands. Hyosuke saw her long, fiery hair, her white eyes and tan skin. He regained focus as an officer closed the sliding door and turned off the light.

'Anata no namae wa nan desu ka?' asked Hyosuke

As her anger dissipated, the woman looked at the man in front of her. Then, her eyes turn emerald-green as she answered, 'Anonasai.'

'What did she say?' asked an officer in Japanese.

'Anonasai, The Head's sister?!' answered another officer in Japanese.

'Dōushite watashinoheya ni iru no?' questioned Anonasai.

The officers looked at each other in surprise. She spoke their language; whatever they say, she could understand.

Hyosuke used hand signals to instruct an officer to watch the hallway, another to oversee the window, and another to listen to the radio. A medic checked the unconscious officer with blood leaking out of his mouth. Anonasai tried to stand but an officer pushed her back down.

'What is it?' asked Hyosuke

'Desk drawer, there is medicine for internal injuries,' answered Anonasai

'Why help us?' questioned an officer behind her in Japanese.

'Blood is hard to remove from carpet, especially white carpet.'

An officer opened the desk drawer to see labelled medicine

in English. Both were needles with clear liquids inside: one was for minor injuries, the other for major. Unfortunately, he couldn't read the label of the latter, so he asked Hyosuke which one it was.

'Migite,' said Anonasai, lifting her right hand.

Hyosuke nodded at the officer and passed the medicine to the medic. The medic took out the needle, injected the officer in the arm, and waited. His breathing slowed with a horrible gargling sound until he took a clear breath and spat out bloody mucus.

'You better clean that up,' hissed Anonasai.

The bloodied officer stared at her with confusion before anger struck, making him draw his Kahr with live ammo. He stormed over to her, held his gun to her head, and spoke too fast for her to understand what was said.

'We need her alive,' reminded Hyosuke in Japanese.

'No, we don't, we're inside the mansion. Everything else is our job,' snapped the officer.

The officer holding Anonasai down backed away as the officer watching the hallway closed the door and reported in. The room stilled, as silence and apprehension took over.

A knock echoed on the white wooden door as a female voice filled the room. 'Anonasai, I have the masks you requested.'

Hyosuke signalled to all officers to stay put. Anonasai looked at the door as all officers readied themselves for what could happen next. 'Thanks, Oxy, leave them there.'

Anticipation filled the room as the silence was deafening.

'Yes, ma'am.'

A small thud is heard before footsteps retreat down the hall. Hyosuke moved towards Anonasai, who went to defend herself, but officers on the stealth team had their weapons trained on her.

'Why help us? You are an assassin.'

'Who said I'm helping you? I could be stalling.'

'You die if you are,' said a male voice behind Hyosuke.

Anonasai braced herself and asked, 'Why are you here? In my room, my clan's home?'

Hyosuke looked into her eyes to see no fear; she focused only on him. 'My team and I are here to arrest The Head and clan members for crimes against Japan.'

She stared back at him before walking to the light switch and making the room light again. A few officers using infrared said a few colourful words as they were blinded.

Hyosuke walked with her as she walked over to her bed and reached under. The stealth team trained their guns on her once more, so did Hyosuke.

'Relax ... it's forbidden to keep weapons in rooms.' Anonasai pulled out a wooden box with gold clips holding it closed. She undid the clasps to reveal a painting kit. 'I can hand over The Head but no one else.'

'No deal,' snapped the bloodied officer.

Hyosuke held up a hand to quieten the officer. 'Why The Head?'

'He is controlling, and his members are on assignments now. Only my members are home, waiting for errands.'

'Great, this mission was for nothing,' moaned one of the Japanese officers.

'Not yet, Officer. Where is The Head now?' queried Hyosuke.

'He is in the ballroom. Down the hall, the seventh door on the right.'

The stealth team rushed out of the room and followed her instructions. Hyosuke watched as the last stealth member left the room before following them. Hyosuke looked back at Anonasai as she painted her mask. Hyosuke breathed out his frustration and followed the stealth team to the ballroom.

There, they saw a man in black clothing with a purple vest and short, fiery red hair standing in the middle of the room playing the violin. He was playing a piece that Hyosuke knew but couldn't name. The beautiful ballroom made the music sound even more enchanting.

The Head stopped abruptly as they entered. 'I said no interruptions.' His voice was cold and harsh.

Hyosuke's team tapped on each other's shoulders, a signal that they were ready, but a figure walked past them. Hyosuke went to grab the figure but he smelt paint and hesitated.

'Apologies, brother, but I ...'

'You, you dare disgrace your mask!' roared The Head.

Anonasai put her hands behind her back and signalled a countdown. 'It was bland, and this suits me best.'

Hyosuke walked forward as she closed her fists and he aimed at The Head's head.

'You are under arrest by ...' started a Japanese stealth member. Officers formed a line beside Hyosuke. Soon blood sprayed from an officer's neck and he fell, lifeless.

'Take cover!' yelled another officer.

'You bastard!' yelled Anonasai with venom.

The Head bowed before throwing the bow with lethal intent. Anonasai caught it and threw it back, piercing the red curtain. A soft *ouch* was heard, injuring the person hiding behind the curtain.

There was silence for a brief period so everyone could find cover. Gunfire soon thundered throughout the ballroom as officers fired where they believed the sniper was hiding. Hyosuke turned over a table and hid behind it; Anonasai joined him.

'Anyone in your clan a sniper?' he asked.

She looked at him before standing and yelling a name that he couldn't hear. Soon all gunfire stopped. Hyosuke stood and called her an idiot as his team soon regrouped with their captain.

'You could've gotten yourself killed,' hissed Hyosuke.

The woman with red hair standing in front of him who

had just risked her life, raised her left eyebrow at him and crossed her arms, saying, 'I doubt that.'

'I am confident the sniper would have shot you and no one else.' Hyosuke stepped closer to her and continued, 'No one can survive a bullet.' He saw her blush before the captain of the stealth team called his attention away. Hyosuke turned around and walked to his team but not without feeling a stinging sensation in his neck. He rubbed his neck twice to see nothing on his hand, but he felt a small bump in the centre. He turned to see if Anonasai was behind him, but she had already disappeared.

*   *   *

Our mission a total bust. The Head in the wind, the mansion reportedly in ashes, and Anonasai, the beautiful fiery redhead, in the wind along with her members, but one thing still bugged me. Why did she help them? Why risk her life and betray her clan? He had time to think about it on the plane back to Japan and wrote up his report. Once he was done with his ten-page report and a condolence letter, he had a drink, ate a fine meal and read a newspaper before falling asleep. He didn't wake until turbulence shook the plane abruptly. Hyosuke looked around in confusion for a short while until he realised that he was still on the plane. He looked at his watch to see the flight was coming to an end. He waited for the plane to land and for the hostess to announce the okay to disembark.

Hyosuke gathered his belongings from the Tokyo International Airport baggage claim carousel, noticing that the airport was extremely busy with foreigners and citizens. He also noticed a delicate fragrance in the air. He looked around the multi-level airport to see cherry blossoms blooming in the airport Zen gardens. He smiled at the small Zen garden before leaving and finding his police vehicle then driving to the Tokyo police headquarters. He walked through the glass doors of his office and was immediately ordered into the field by his supervisor.

Four adolescents had robbed a store. Hyosuke sped to the location and was shocked to see stampeding citizens fleeing the shopping centre. He entered the shopping centre through the back door and searched the building floor by floor. He radioed in his findings. 'Level One clear.' Hyosuke searched the second level for ten minutes, then radioed, 'Level Two clear.' He did the same on the third level for ten minutes before he radioed, 'Level Three clear.' Hyosuke moved to the fourth level where he found the four adolescents tied in the middle of the tiled walkway. He moved to a concrete pillar nearby and whispered to the nearest boy in Japanese, 'Oi, what happened?'

The boy lifted his head and started to shake; tears fell uncontrollably as he looked around. A young boy next to him tried to reassure him, to keep him quiet, but something had him terrified. 'Help … Help us!' yelped the young boy. Hyosuke signalled to the boy to keep his voice down; that's when he heard heels clopping on the tiled floor and approaching in front of him. Hyosuke revealed his position to the figure dressed in black. The face was obscured by shadow, but he had a pretty good idea who it was, as the person stopped.

'You're free to go, boys,' stated Hyosuke, aiming his black dragon at the figure. Two boys wriggled themselves about but struggled with the twine.

'Robbery is now a get-out-of-jail crime? You can't be serious,' retorted the figure.

Hyosuke stood his ground as he listened to the female's voice. First, it gave him chills, but then the stance and the arms crossed were familiar. The boys were still struggling to free themselves until a thread of twine snapped. Mixed feelings filled the air, but the boys soon got up and ran. Hyosuke made a radio call and listened to the hurried footsteps dissolving into the hall behind him and into the custody of officers waiting outside. His radio soon came alive again; however, he switched it off as he held the figure at gunpoint. He had a hunch, so he yelled, 'Remove the hood!'

The figure revealed her mask and red hair; Hyosuke relaxed and let his guard down. She saw this. She wasn't prepared to go to jail; not yet. While he wasn't paying attention, Anonasai ran to the handrail and jumped over it. He yelled at her to stop and reached out to grab her, but he failed. He closed his eyes, dreading to see a body, dreading to hear the dull thud of the impact.

Hyosuke turned away from the soon-to-be-crime scene only to hear a female voice call his name. Hyosuke turned back to see Anonasai standing below him, waving at him. She had no injuries. However, the marble ground under her was cracked and caved in. He didn't know why he returned the gesture. This was only the beginning of their run-ins.

*   *   *

Hyosuke had just finalised his last report for the night. He walked out of his office and was walking home when a high alert made his phone blink red. He then hurried back, putting on a bulletproof vest and an armband before going to a briefing room. As he walked through the threshold, he was pulled away.

'Officer Hyosuke, you are to go on this mission as a negotiation officer.'

He looked at his commanding officer. It had been years since he'd been a negotiation officer, but he was still the best at it. Soon he saw his fellow officers run to their assigned vehicles, so he also ran to his vehicle. Hyosuke sat in the driver side of a dark blue and white Honda NXS Gen 11 police series vehicle. They were commanded to drive to Umeda Station, Ōsaka.

As traffic cleared, Hyosuke flicked a switch in the centre console of his car. His vehicle hovered in the sky for five minutes before taking off towards Ōsaka. What would have been a six-hour drive, ended up only taking twenty minutes. As he arrived, he saw utter chaos. People were running in different directions, screaming and pushing; personal belongings littered the pavement as he walked to the entrance. He noticed that fellow officers had cleared the area and stationed themselves nearby down the stairs to Umeda's first platform. A white and aqua shinkansen had stopped at a siding, blue lights illuminating off the track to show that it was still hovering above the tracks. Hyosuke saw a young man wearing a brown jumper, brown pants and white joggers staring at the train. The platform was spotless, despite all the chaos he saw moments earlier. Hyosuke stepped onto the platform to see the young man looking at his reflection in the window until he turned his attention to the entrance and saw Hyosuke. His eyes were cold, lifeless and dark.

Hyosuke looked into the shinkansen to see it was empty, but a shadow caught his eye. He knew who the shadow was as he started to negotiate. 'Sir, let's talk. Tell me what you doing.'

No response.

The young man looked at Officer Hyosuke before shifting his attention back to the train's window.

'Why is the train important?' asked Hyosuke. That's when the young man snapped his attention to Officer Hyosuke and pulled his jumper to one side. Hyosuke saw multiple wires and half a small screen with a countdown. *So, was the shinkansen the bomb? Or was the young man the bomb?* Hyosuke went radio silent and looked for the shadow; however, it was nowhere to be seen. *Am I seeing things?* That's when he saw a dark figure behind the young man, about to strike. 'Tell me, young man, why are you here today and in Ōsaka?'

That's when the young man came to life; his eyes went wide as he outstretched his arms, revealing the full vest strapped to his chest. 'We henchmen will have imperialism back. This shinkansen will be the beginning of our plan,' replied the young man in Japanese.

Hyosuke paled as he saw the timer getting closer to zero. With no idea what the bomb's radius could be, he started to feel sick. However, time began to increase as the young man spoke.

'Beginning of what?' asked Hyosuke calmly.

'We henchmen will have imperialism back ...'

With a raised hand, Hyosuke signalled for the young man to stop. He didn't want to hear the same nonsense again, but perhaps talking would buy him, and everyone else, time. 'Sorry, go on,' apologised Officer Hyosuke.

'We henchmen will have imperialism back. This shinkansen will be the beginning of our plan.'

Hyosuke looked at the timer to see time had increased by a

minute, so he looked at the shinkansen. On the outside it was an ordinary shinkansen. He needed to inspect the interior. As Hyosuke opened his mouth to ask another question, the young man's body lent forward; his eyes rolled back before he hit the ground, revealing a foreign object in the back of his neck. Hyosuke saw the black figure standing before them. Before he could move, the figure tossed a small black box into the growing pool of blood.

Hyosuke stared at the dark figure. 'Anonasai.'

'You're welcome, Officer Hyosuke.'

'We can't keep meeting like this.'

'Why? It's the only time I see you.'

'I'm working,' stated Hyosuke as he cuffed Anonasai's right arm, but she moved out of his grasp. He watched as she circled him. She was toying with him. *If it were anyone else, I'd pull out my taser gun, but we have a bond now … yet again. But I'm done with her little game.* That's when he remembered; he'd had radio silence for too long. He turned his radio back on and reported in his status, the suspect was dead … and that he had one in custody.

'Killjoy,' whispered Anonasai in his ear. But she went willingly as he walked her out to the street. Cameras flashed as journalists grabbed pictures of the terrorist and the hero officer who saved Ōsaka. Two officers then appeared among the flashing lights to take her away, however Hyosuke refused their offer and took Anonasai to his vehicle. He opened the back passenger door, put her in, then walked to the driver's side. He drove fifteen minutes from the scene before handcuffs flew into the front passenger seat. He pulled into the emergency lane and stopped.

'Ki wa tashika desu ka!?' shouted Hyosuke as he turned to see the back seats were empty.

'I'm not crazy … and I told you to put seatbelts back here,' scolded Anonasai as she climbed back onto the seat. She looked at Hyosuke before asking, 'Why didn't you hand me over to the other police officers?'

'You are not one of the henchmen. You are one of the Makino and you might have answers … and I couldn't hand over my friend.'

Anonasai leaned closer to him and whispered, 'We both know we're more than friends.'

Hyosuke looked at her lips, then drew his attention back to her eyes before turning to face the road; he refocused before driving. She spoke the truth, so he went to his apartment and took her with him. Anonasai took off her shoes and put on house shoes before following Hyosuke inside. His apartment had dark wooden flooring and Akiko screen doors surrounding the lounge room, with another folding screen door leading to the bedroom.

'How do you know where to find me?' asked Hyosuke.

'Don't start with boring questions. I planted a tracker on you.'

Hyosuke emptied his pockets before placing a hand on the back of his neck. He thought about the odd neck pain at the mansion and realised that it wasn't the pain doctors put down to burnout and age, it was her shooting her tracker into his neck. 'That's an invasion of my …'

'You invaded my privacy when you broke into my bedroom.'

Hyosuke looked at her for a while before ordering her it take it out. She stared at him then he snapped, 'Now!', which seemed to get her moving. She hated being ordered around but he would no longer have a GPS tracker in him. He felt her bone-chilling fingers on his warm skin then a pinch.

'What do you know of the Torimaki?' asked Hyosuke

'Really? You can't let go off work for five minutes.'

'Anonasai … please.'

Anonasai sighed, saying 'The Torimaki want the old Japan back with the curfews and tougher laws. The black box that your fellow police officers have will tell you everything.'

Hyosuke turned to face Anonasai; her cheeks reddened as he closed the gap between them.

'You know more than that.'

'I do.'

She took a step back; he knew if he let her out of his sight, she'd disappear again. Without thinking, he grabbed her hand, looked into her green eyes and lost himself in them. He placed his other hand around her waist. She allowed him to do so as she placed her hands on his chest. She looked at his lips as he moved in and kissed her. She kissed him back. Anonasai then moved her arms around Hyosuke's neck when he stopped. He gazed into her eyes yet again and saw her cheeks blushing, their breaths mixing as they stared into each other's eyes with unspoken words before kissing once again. They headed to the bedroom, where they removed each other's clothing.

CHAPTER 20

yosuke was jolted awake as the truck suddenly stopped. He looked around to see that a new day had dawned with soft orange colours streaking across the sky. Through the front windscreen he saw a ten-car line-up in front of their vehicle. *When did they arrive? How long had they been here?*

'Into the back,' ordered The Head.

Hyosuke looked behind the truck to see more vehicles approaching. 'We will be seen.'

The Head pinched the bridge of his nose in frustration before saying, 'Centre seat folds down.'

Anonasai folded the centre seat down and Hyosuke climbed in, bringing his belongings with him.

'Constantine?'

'What?'

'Do you still have your universal silencer?' asked Anonasai.

Constantine reached under his seat, pulled out the silencer and handed it to her.

'One last thing.'

'Hurry up!' hissed Constantine, looking over his shoulder.

'How does my arse look?'

Constantine growled and muttered under his breath as he turned his attention to the front of the vehicle; however, Valentin silently chuckled. Anonasai lifted the centre seat, making the hidden compartment dark once more. Ping made the side panels mirror the outside surroundings.

'Where is my arrowslit?' asked Anonasai.

'Pardon?' queried Sasha.

'Behind Dad. An arrowslit is a narrow vertical reinforcement through which an archer can launch arrows, or a crossbowman can launch bolts,' explained Ping.

Hyosuke looked at Ping, surprised she had called him 'Dad'; they'd decided to keep their relationship private. Anonasai moved around Hyosuke to see a small black handle, so she pulled it to reveal her arrowslit. As the truck moved closer to the borderline, they saw a white concrete box and fifteen guards.

The guards spoke in Escaian to Valentin. Sasha could only make out very little of the conversation in the hidden compartment. Ping sent out an EMP that fried electronic devices. She then hacked into the town's system's mainframe and searched the scanning system for any images of their vehicle and their information.

'Ping, how is your tech working?' asked Hyosuke.

'I made the EMP target certain systems. If not, we all would be in custody by now.'

'Talking will certainly get us caught if you two will not shut it,' snapped Anonasai. She looked out of her arrowslit once more to see a power generator. 'Kuroi dragon wo shi te kudasai.'

Hyosuke looked hard at Anonasai as she held her right hand out. He eventually handed over his gun and she screwed the universal silencer on, then waited for a signal.

CHAPTER 21

Soldiers approached the truck and opened the doors. Valentin looked at his fellow soldiers with respect while Constantine looked down at the soldiers in their camouflage uniforms with matching hats. Behind them were soldiers handling automatic weapons that could switch from stun to lethal with the press of a button, and behind them were a line of dog kennels. The German Shepherds looked happy in their huge kennels.

'Papers,' demanded a soldier in Escaian.

Valentin handed over his passport and foreign minister papers. In contrast, Constantine handed over a fake passport, which stated he was Leo Pendragon, a journalist reporting a news story when chaos erupted but had been pulled out of the field as a developing story was occurring in Belarus.

'Why you travel with Minister Valentin?' enquired a solider

'Coincidentally, we're going to the same country.'

'And you, sir, why are you travelling to Belarus?' questioned another solider in Escaian.

'To see my brother.'

A soldier yelled out that all the equipment was down. Clipboards soon came out as visual checks started. Next, dogs were released with their handlers; they approached the truck and sniffed around, then moved away as their noses were irritated by the limes. Finally, a soldier opened the back of the vehicle and quickly dodged the rolling limes as they gave way to gravity.

'Clear!' reported a soldier after saying a few colourful words.

'Why do you have limes?' asked another soldier.

Constantine looked at Valentin to answer, but he was taking too long, not to mention the silence was getting to him. *Would the soldier detain them if he took too long to answer?*

Constantine received his papers back and as he returned them under the sun visor, he pressed a small button. Soon the power generator exploded, catching all the soldiers' attention.

'Sima and Caipirinha, my brother he makes …' began Valentin.

'Too slow, you idiot,' muttered Constantine.

'You're clear to go,' announced one of the soldiers as he waved the truck over the border.

Valentin breathed a sigh of relief as he drove into Belarus. He didn't look back at the commotion behind them, or Escya.

He drove ten kilometres, then fifteen when The Head told him to stop. Constantine pressed the button in the sun visor twice before getting out. He walked beside the vehicle, stopped at the rear, and waited. Valentin joined him as the side passenger door swung violently open.

'Why are you waiting here?' questioned Valentin.

'I dare say my sister will have something to say. She always does.'

'I drove fifteen kilometres before stopping. Why?'

'So she would calm down.'

Valentin looked behind him as a commotion started. He saw Sasha talking to Anonasai, trying to keep her calm, *but why?* Ping was helping Hyosuke with a bloody nose. *Oh, was that why she was angry? I didn't take off that fast. I stopped suddenly, yes, but was her anger appropriate?*

'Anonasai, what is the matter? Why are you so filled with venom that my Sasha cannot extinguish your fire?'

Valentin noted that Anonasai's eyes were green, not white. *So, she wasn't murderous. No, but she could be lethal, and maybe Sasha was calming her down.*

'I know why Constantine Knight did not want me in that hidden compartment. He knew I could save myself, save Hyosuke. Ping saved Sasha. Then, the truck braked, and the front wall moved towards us,' snapped Anonasai with malice.

Valentin looked at Constantine with fury, as his angel,

his wife, was in a death trap. He clenched his fists but he gave into his anger and swung. He struck Constantine on the jaw, knocking him out. Sasha heard bones breaking and stopped holding Anonasai back. She went to her husband to see him looking at The Head's unconscious body. Valentin then walked to the side of the truck to Hyosuke and Ping.

'How did you break your nose?' asked Valentin.

'Elbow to the nose,' replied Hyosuke, still holding his nose.

'Is The Head …?' asked Ping.

'No, give it five minutes, and he will be all right,' answered Sasha.

Hyosuke unholstered his black dragon and aimed it at Anonasai, who looked at him with concern. She heard footsteps and a clicking of the jaw. So, she stared down the barrel of the gun until it fired. She dodged to the left and, looking behind her, saw her brother with a head wound. Hyosuke holstered his weapon once more and said to The Head, 'That's for trying to kill my family.'

Valentin nodded in agreement.

'Now what? We can't leave him here,' urged Ping.

'Sure, we can get in,' replied Valentin.

'He'll wake in a few hours,' stated Sasha.

'With a headache,' suggested Valentin, sniggering.

'Stop clowning around!' hissed Ping in annoyance.

Anonasai and Hyosuke chuckled before realising Ping didn't understand their history.

'Can we fix the compartment, so it's not a death trap?' asked Sasha.

All eyes were on Anonasai, and she smiled wickedly. With the help of Hyosuke, Anonasai lifted her brother's body into the rear end of the truck after releasing the limes. She looked around for ropes or anything to keep her brother in one place when two belts hit the steel floor. She didn't ask questions as she secured her brother and closed the back curtain from curious eyes.

CHAPTER 22

Valentin arrived at the Belarusian airport and drove to an undisclosed location where he and Anonasai checked up on Constantine while Ping worked on their passports. Valentin moved the curtain aside to see Constantine death-staring at them as he was still restrained.

'Where have you taken us?' demanded Constantine.

Anonasai laughed. 'It sucks not being in control, must feel awful.'

'Careful. The bastard is bound – untie him, and he'll lash out,' warned Valentin.

'Actually, Valentin,' Constantine shook his hands, making the belts fall to the ground, 'I could've escaped at any time.' He straightened his suit and vest.

'Why wait till now?' asked Valentin, shocked.

Constantine looked at Valentin with superiority. 'For the look on your face.'

Anonasai rolled her eyes then grabbed her brother by the collar and threw him against the back wall, making a dent in it. 'Stop being an arse and get moving. Ping and the others are waiting for us at the entrance.'

Anonasai jumped down from the back compartment and walked off. Valentin put his hands up in defence before following her to the entrance. Sasha hugged her husband then smiled at Anonasai. 'Where is The Head?'

'He's coming,' answered Hyosuke with a subtle nod towards the road.

Ping, Sasha, Valentin and Anonasai looked down the road and saw him coming, but he looked different. His vest and cream clothes were the same, but his face looked different.

'Where did those shades come from?' asked Anonasai.

'Jealous, are we?'

'Of you? Don't be silly.'

'If you must know, I got them off a gentleman lying in the grass.'

Anonasai shuddered and walked inside. Ping inserted a new implant in The Head's wrist and followed Anonasai. The blue tiled floor was relaxing after what they had been through the last few days. The air smelled of coconut and mangos. Extinct fish and marine mammals were projected swimming around on the roof while relaxing ocean sounds filled the air. Staff members were wearing aqua uniforms that blended well with the ocean theme.

They queued up for tickets for South Row Airport and lingered for three hours. Finally, Anonasai sat on a coral-themed lounge and waited for Ping, Sasha and Valentin to join her.

'Anonasai, a word in private,' whispered Sasha. Anonasai followed Sasha away from the others.

'Ping, who is your mother travelling as?' asked Valentin.

'Miss Kaisøn.'

'And Hyosuke is the same?'

'Yes. You and Sasha are the same. Only The Head is different.'

'Oh?'

'He is travelling as Mick O'Neil.'

'Not Pendragon?'

'No, he isn't royalty.'

Anonasai and Sasha walked back and sat back down as Hyosuke and Constantine joined them.

'Ping, you changed my fake passport,' grumbled Constantine.

'Yes, you are not royalty.'

'When I assigned you on this errand you were to use your … ability to aid the Makino and others, not change my passport,' hissed The Head, pinning Ping with a death stare.

Anonasai looked at Ping as she lowered her head in submission.

'Ping, hold your head up high with honour,' said Hyosuke.

'My clan members will not listen to your nonsense,' snapped The Head, glaring at Hyosuke.

Anonasai flicked Constantine's right ear, making it bleed. 'I will not tell you again. Watch your tone around my daughter.'

Ping looked at Anonasai to see her eyes were white. She loved her mother and father, but The Head not so much. He was always hard on her. He had the same eye colour as Anonasai but always denied being a relation of hers.

So, Ping lent towards her mother and whispered, 'Anonasai, is The Head related to you?'

Anonasai nodded. 'The Head ... Constantine, is my brother.'

'*Flight 447 South Row Airport, America now boarding,*' announced a woman via a hologram.

Anonasai stayed seated as the others went to the gate before following the line of people onto a blue concourse and boarding the Boeing 1000. She sat next to Hyosuke and Ping.

'Everything okay?' checked Ping.

'We've been followed.'

Hyosuke glared at Anonasai. 'Don't be paranoid.'

'When have I been paranoid?'

'Three times in Kyoto and now,' replied Hyosuke.

'Who is following us?' asked Ping.

'A man I have seen before. He is four aisles ahead of us, second seat,' answered Anonasai.

169

CHAPTER 23

The white Boeing 1000, with its boomerang shape and twin engines next to the tail, looked brand new, even though it had had fifty years of service. A blue and purple flag was painted on its tail. It soon took off and Ping waited for the plane to level out before walking down the central aisle to the fourth row ahead of them. She looked on both sides, seeing unfamiliar faces until she saw a man with dark skin, brown eyes and black hair. He wore a black suit with a white shirt underneath. Either way, he stood out from the other passengers.

As Ping returned to her seat, she spotted two more suspicious-looking people in dark suits — one female, dark-skinned with long, black wavy hair and a blonde-haired man with blue eyes. Ping saw Hyosuke reading a holographic newspaper and her mother playing with her medium-length nails, cleaning out the dirt that wasn't there. Ping smiled as she sat down.

'Anonasai isn't paranoid. There are three of them,' Ping relayed to Hyosuke.

'Where?' asked Hyosuke, sighing.

'One four rows up front and the other two are sitting two rows behind us.'

Anonasai had been listening and handed over her phone to Ping. 'Hack into the booking records and find out who they are, please.'

Ping took the phone and started to work her magic. Suddenly, she looked behind her and then back at Hyosuke and Anonasai with a surprised expression.

'What is it?' asked Hyosuke and Anonasai in unison.

'MI5 … what did you do?'

'What *hasn't* your mother done,' whispered Hyosuke sarcastically.

Anonasai glared at him. 'Shush you. Who are the agents, Ping?'

'Agent Noah Bondi, Agent Dan Sharp and Agent Rem Hitchcock.'

Anonasai looked at her phone to ensure Ping's data was accurate, not that she ever doubted her.

'Agent Bondi is dead. I shot him in the chest.'

Hyosuke took Anonasai's phone from Ping, turned on the camera, held it overhead and snapped. He then looked at the photo to see Agent Bondi and Agent Rem Hitchcock exactly two rows behind them.

'He looks alive to me,' Hyosuke pointed out.

Anonasai peered over her seat to see that Rem Hitchcock was in her chair, but Agent Bondi was not. Anonasai looked at the photo again to see that he was there. Something started tapping her shoulder, so she took a deep breath to calm her nerves. She gradually turned to see Agent Bondi in the aisle beside her.

Noah leaned in close. 'Sorry to bother, madam. I couldn't help but notice that the man next to you was taking a photo. For my protection and yours, I request that you remove the photo from your device. Immediately.'

Anonasai looked at Agent Bondi who was now down at her level, holding her gaze. A mistake on his part because she could easily take him out. However, Anonasai held Noah's stare as she deleted the photo. Agent Bondi straightened and walked away. She stared at the chair in front of her before looking at the image she was ordered to delete.

'What are you doing?' asked Hyosuke.

'Investigating.'

'You're being paranoid again, and that picture is gone.'

'Is it?' Anonasai smirked before pocketing her phone. Hyosuke was still on his first holographic newspaper. Ping had hacked into the tablet in front of her to access more options without paying. Across the opposite aisle Sasha was reading a chemistry e-book. Valentin was asleep while Constantine looked as entertained as Anonasai was. They couldn't rest without revisiting memories of that unforgettable day of fire and smoke.

Anonasai shook her head then scanned the tablet in front of her to search the movies and shows available before switching to see how long the flight had left – nine hours.

'Attention all passengers, this is your captain speaking. Lunch will be served shortly. After lunch we will be entering a quiet zone and for this period of time, we request you rest.'

* * *

It wasn't long before Anonasai found herself staring into the darkness. She reclined her chair and held herself tight as the darkness moved in waves. She looked around for Hyosuke and Ping to pull her out, but they did not. She reached out for someone – anything – to secure herself, to reassure herself that she was safe. That's when the darkness shifted again to fire and smoke, wooden and mortar homes burning down, bodies burning alive, people screaming. Smoke was suffocating her. Her breathing became rapid as more images emerged. Hyosuke pushed up his armrest and cuddled her. He stroked her hair and kissed her head until the lights came back on.

CHAPTER 24

Noah Bondi looked around in his dark space and saw a green blinking light next to him, so he reached out for it. It was cold and flexible. It was Remmy's tech glasses. He was on first watch and had nothing better to do so he put on her glasses. They came alive without a password and he was surprised that they soon went to night-vision mode. He looked around and checked the resting heart rhythms.

He saw Anonasai and Hyosuke sleeping together like a married couple. He smiled at the young woman beside them. Her name was blurred out but that didn't worry him. Noah walked up to Dan Sharp's row before turning around and walking down to the fourth row yet again where he saw Sasha and Valentin Silca, and a Mick O'Neil.

'Quit staring, it's disturbing, Agent,' said Mick O'Neil softly.

Agent Bondi jumped as the man had a resting heartbeat but he spoke. Mick O'Neil took his sleeping mask off and looked at Noah.

'You can see in the dark? How?' questioned Agent Bondi.

Mick O'Neil signalled for Noah to move back before moving to the aisle. 'You have Rem Hitchcock's glasses on but I doubt they give you the full colour spectrum, or the truth.'

'Oh, you're not O'Neil. You're Constantine Knight,' surmised Noah, and he gestured for Constantine to follow him. They walked to the back of Business Class so they could talk freely.

'In the flesh. Now what are you doing staring at people while they sleep?' questioned Constantine.

'I don't answer to you, I answer to the king.'

'Ah yes, that old line. I too used to answer to a king but he got old and he died. God bless his soul.'

Agent Bondi looked at Constantine before asking, 'Which king?'

'King Charles II … before your time.'

Noah's glasses filled up with information about King Charles II, a plague, a great fire, civil war then exile. He didn't read all the information, just the key words. 'Must be hard to follow a king who is exiled.' said Noah.

'Even harder to follow a dead one, not to mention a fake one,' retorted Constantine.

Agent Bondi frowned at Constantine. He always had a

comeback, but to insult the royal line was going too far. 'The king is not a fake.'

'Believe it or not is up to you. Many royal lines died out long ago. Some couldn't manage the fact that their family line was ending and desperately tried to produce heirs. The Lennon line is not that of blue blood.'

'How did you survive a bullet to the heart, Agent?'

'Spies don't reveal their secrets.'

'It wouldn't be a bulletproof vest with tracing technology that gives the wearer the appearance that they have been shot, would it?'

Noah growled in annoyance before walking back to his seat. Constantine walked past shortly after. Agent Bondi nudged Rem to wake up and begin her watch. 'I'm awake,' slurred Rem.

'Good, your turn to take watch.'

'Why are you so grumpy? We're in the quiet part of travel.'

'I encountered Constantine from the Escaian bunker.'

'Oh really?' Rem replied with a hint of excitement in her voice.

Noah returned the tech glasses before putting on his sleeping mask. Rem checked the passengers' sleep rhythms and observed all was normal except for one. She saw the time and was woken up half an hour early. *That will keep.* However, she saw a new search history and brought it up to see King Charles II. On the seat in front of her, she projected Anna

Knight's past that she had gathered, *but what tied her and the late king together?*

Rem saw a staff member walking down the aisle, checking on everyone. He stopped beside her and said, 'Madam, this is the quiet period …' Rem showed her MI5 badge, which soon shut him up. 'Front row seat A3 is also MI5. He is my colleague. Leave him be for an hour and a half.'

The staff member nodded. Agent Rem reviewed her history lesson before her glasses start to alarm her of an abnormality. She disabled her projector function to see someone's heart rhythm racing. She looked at the name to see Miss Korosu Kaisøn. MI5 and many other countries needed her alive, so Rem left her seat and went to see Korosu Kaisøn sweating and breathing rapidly. Rem crouched down and slightly nudged her.

'You will leave my sister alone.'

Rem turned to see a man she had seen before but who looked different in infrared. 'Apologies, sir.'

Rem reached for her glasses and pressed a button three times. Now she could see the man like it was daytime. His fiery red hair was neat, and his cream clothing was clean, but he smelt of limes and coconut; his left sleeve had recently been sewn back together. His eyes weren't green like they were in the bunker; they were white. *Is that how he is seeing in the dark?* she wondered before saying his name softly, 'Constantine.'

'Rem Hitchcock, so you're working with MI5.'

'And a few others,' she said nonchalantly.

'A busy woman.' Constantine smiled. 'What do you want with my sister?'

'Sorry, that's classified, unless you give me something. Follow me and we'll talk.'

'You dare bargain with me?' he toyed.

Agent Rem walked to the back end of the aisle and waited for only one minute before a figure emerged from the dark, but the figure wasn't Constantine. Instead, it was another passenger heading to the lavatory. She sighed in defeat. She had seen and heard Dan and Noah use that technique over and over, and it was successful for them, but here she was, waiting alone. So, she decided to head back to her seat and do further research as to where she went wrong. Rem reviewed video after video of agents using the same technique; they all persuaded the target to follow them to the required location, *so where did I go wrong?* She thought about this for a while until, suddenly, the timer in her tech glasses went off. She now had to go to Dan and wake him up. The lights slowly started to come back on. 'Wake up. It's your turn to watch.'

'All right,' Dan replied, half asleep.

'Also, I tried the bargaining technique, but it didn't work.'

Dan was confused until he realised what she was talking about. 'You mean negotiate? We don't bargain. Where did you go, Rem?'

'To the end of the aisle.'

Dan looked behind him; there was the back where the lavatory was, then there was the very back where it was quiet. He didn't have to ask where Rem chose to negotiate. 'To negotiate, go to a hospitable environment, not next to a goddamn lavatory.'

Rem looked towards the back of the plane and saw where she went wrong, then she walked away without a word. Agent Sharp looked around for the tech glasses he was supposed to wear for his watch, but he knew that when Rem was in a mood, it was best to leave her alone. So, he did his watch the old-fashioned way by walking up the aisle in the dim light. He reached the end of the aisle, turned around, and nearly knocked a steward over as he was close behind him.

'Apologies, sir, the resting period is at an end. I request you return to your seat.'

'Dude, I nearly killed your arse. Don't follow so close behind me. You nearly gave me a heart attack.'

The steward apologised before walking away. Dan returned to his seat and pulled out his book as the lights soon brightened.

CHAPTER 25

Ping woke first and looked around to see her father cuddling her mother, who was asleep. *When was the last time my mother slept like this?* She looked peaceful and happy, not exhausted. Hyosuke stirred at the sudden loudness.

'Dad, when did that happen?' asked Ping, watching her mother sleeping.

'This rarely happens and when it does, she usually screams, but this time she didn't.'

'Why?'

'Anonasai is haunted by her memories.'

Ping looked at her mother once more with sadness. 'To revisit the same scene repeatedly must be torture for her.' Ping must have stared for too long, as her mother's eyes shot open. Ping jumped back into her seat before apologising.

Anonasai looked around at her surroundings quickly as Hyosuke calmed her by softly stroking her head. 'You are still on the plane. Ping and I are here with you.'

Anonasai's eyes turned from white to green as she heard his voice. She focused on his voice and slowed her breathing. Then she looked at Hyosuke and Ping. 'I told you never to let me fall asleep.'

'You needed it. You're not so exhausted now.'

'Ping, did anything happen?' asked Anonasai.

Ping shook her head as turbulence shook the plane.

Attention passengers, this is your captain speaking.

Anonasai rolled her eyes at his timing; his deep voice irritated her.

We are starting our descent to South Row Airport. I ask that you buckle yourselves in, and again, we thank you for flying with Belarusian Airlines.

Anonasai looked at the tablet in front of her to see that the plane was close to landing. She felt happy that this mission was over. Finally, she could drive her Honda NSX back home, take a long hot bath and get rid of her black hair. Constantine could have hair-dye remover with him. She scoffed at the thought. *Of course not, he never dyed his hair as that is forbidden in the Makino clan.* She was free now to do whatever she wanted as a rogue.

Then she thought about Hyosuke as he would return to Japan where he had business to take care of. Then there was

Ping who would return to the Makino clan and continue her work. Valentin and Sasha would find a place unknown to her, and Constantine would continue leading the Makino clan.

Anonasai wiped a tear from her eye. Hyosuke saw this but didn't respond. Turbulence shook the plane as it landed on the tarmac. Passengers slowly stood and formed a line to walk onto the concourse. That's when she heard them.

'Are they ready?' enquired Bondi.

Rem nodded. 'Yes, officers are in place. It's all up to you and Agent Sharp from here.'

'And local PD?' asked Noah.

'Standing by. Should we be having this conversation? What if the target can hear us?'

'I doubt she can.'

Anonasai paid no attention and kept her focus forward as the line of passengers started to move.

'Her brother can see in the dark. Nothing is a surprise,' commented Agent Rem.

Anonasai moved with the line of people down the concourse into South Row Airport. The airport looked precisely as the same. She liked this airport — *a little time capsule from the past, only renovations were slowly destroying its history.* The only new addition in the display section was the 1928 red Lockheed 5B Vega safely hanging from the ceiling with industrial wire and a McDonnell Douglas F/A-18 Hornet. *The aircrafts are a nice addition to the airport to show the difference between commercial and air force planes, but they needed the Hinkel He 178 to really show off aircraft evolution.*

Anonasai wanted to look at the exhibits all day but home was calling her, so she walked over to the baggage collection and waited for her red sports bag. That's when she remembered the agents' plan. Anonasai handed her phone to Ping as her bag came into view. Ping looked at the phone's screen to see a blue arrow pointing east. She shrunk the screen and a green dot was shown. *But why? Why give this to me?*

'Everything okay?' asked Ping.

Anonasai didn't reply as she pulled out her mask and hid it under her hood. Hyosuke rushed over. 'There are ten police cars outside and twenty unmarked …'

'I know, courtesy of the agents on my tail.'

Hyosuke looked worryingly at Anonasai as he knew one day this would happen. Unfortunately, there weren't many escape routes in the airport, especially not one that had been renovated recently. Anonasai handed her red sports bag to Ping, saying, 'Look after this. It'll lead you where you need to go.'

Ping looked at the red sports bag then back at her mother. 'I hate it when you say stuff like that.'

Anonasai saw Agent Sharp and Agent Bondi approaching. She slipped on her mask, nodded at Hyosuke, then ran towards the VIP lounge.

CHAPTER 26

Dan and Noah exited the concourse as Rem debriefed the local police officers on the plan. They walked to baggage collection and spotted their target talking to two civilians and putting on her well-known mask. She saw them and ran.

'Mother f....' uttered Noah, giving chase

'No, you can't say that ... only I can say that!' snapped Dan.

'Fine, then you say it.'

'Nope, moment's gone.'

They followed Anonasai to the VIP lounge where she weaved through the crowd. Noah yelled at civilians to move out of their way as he closed in on her. That was until she changed her direction, and he ran straight into a fountain.

Dan left his partner behind as he followed the target back to the baggage collection, weaving in and out of the crowd. Anonasai jumped onto the moving conveyer belt. Her momentum grew faster as the conveyer belt aided her. She leapt over large and small bags with ease and jumped off as the conveyor belt came to a bend. People screamed in shock and dived out of her way. Anonasai ran towards a crowded food court. Dan couldn't afford to lose her, but he didn't know if he could continue this foot pursuit much longer. She turned quickly to a busier section of the airport, and that's when Dan had had enough. He unholstered his gun and fired at the roof.

Citizens ducked, screamed and hit the floor, trying to make themselves small. Mothers and fathers shielded their children. Anonasai saw this so she stopped dead in her tracks before turning around to see Dan walking towards her, gun drawn.

'By order of King Sirray Lennon, Anonasai, wandering assassin, you are under arrest,' yelled Dan.

Anonasai stared at the agent as he approached. Dread filled her as he walked closer and closer until a black object fell between them. Smoke quickly filled the air. She could hear the agent coughing. A flashback froze her to the spot as the smoke consumed them. She stood for what seemed like hours until a firm grip grabbed her arm and pulled her away from the smoke. As her vision cleared, she saw Constantine beside her and Sasha looking behind them.

'What are you doing?' shouted Anonasai.

'Saving you,' confirmed Constantine.

Anonasai ripped her arm free. 'I don't need your help!'

'Oh please, running around like a child is not escaping. Besides, this is Sasha's last act for the Makino.'

Anonasai looked at Sasha, who was holding black balls of material in her hands. Anonasai couldn't trust her brother's word, not after her banishment. 'Are you true to your word, brother?'

'Of course. Sasha will be removed from the Makino clan after this.'

Sasha threw another smoke bomb before catching up with Anonasai and The Head. She ran with them to a section of the airport where civilians were taking cover. Anonasai slid on her mask then sat with her brother and Sasha on the floor.

'Where are Hyosuke and Ping?' asked Sasha.

Anonasai smiled. 'Don't worry about them. They should be in my car and long gone from here.'

'Smart,' praised Constantine.

Before Sasha could have her say, green emergency doors swung open revealing two police officers and Agent Bondi with wet hair and wearing a new suit. Constantine looked over his shoulder and saw officers combing through the crowd. 'Any ideas, sister, before you are taken away?'

'Funny.' Anonasai noticed that the room had bulletproof glass, and the only way out was past the police officers and through the emergency doors.

'Sasha, do you still have a smoke bomb?' whispered Anonasai.

'Just one. What are you thinking?'

'I need you to throw it over to that large group of people,' directed Anonasai.

Sasha looked at the targeted group of people before looking back at her friend. 'Then what?'

'Now, Sasha!' ordered Anonasai.

Sasha looked at the police officers and agents in the room to ensure they weren't watching her. She threw the smoke bomb at the targeted group of people and watched as the black ball disappeared into the group, covering them in smoke. Sasha heard them coughing as the agents and police officers rushed over. She turned her attention to Anonasai but she had disappeared. She looked around the space and at The Head — his eyes were white. He didn't say a word as he pointed towards the rafters.

Butterflies filled Sasha's stomach as an officer walked over to them and asked them for identification. Constantine showed the officer the implant on his wrist. 'What's that?' asked an officer.

'That, Officer Cunnings, is my identification.'

Officer Cunnings radioed for Officer Whippet to assist. Whippet walked over with a tablet and wand, and checked the man's wrist. Then, he waited for the imagery to load. 'Mick O'Neil, you're free to go.'

Sasha showed Officer Whippet her implant on her wrist next and waited.

'Sasha Silca, you're free to go.'

Sasha and Constantine walked out the emergency doors to the airport's main area and made their way to the exit.

'Did you make my warrants disappear?' asked Sasha.

'What warrants?'

'Don't toy with me.'

'I had one of my people remove your history from the Makino clan. Anything you do from here is on you, Sasha.'

Constantine signalled Sasha to stop as Anonasai appeared in front of them. The ground under her fractured with the impact. Anonasai smiled at her brother and Sasha before exiting through the main entrance.

CHAPTER 27

'Freeze! This is the South Row Police Department!' yelled a male voice.

His voice was loud and made Anonasai, Constantine and Sasha stop in their tracks. Anonasai looked around to see civilians behind barricades protected by many police officers. She scanned their faces to see none were familiar to her. She wasn't armed. She couldn't say the same for her brother or Sasha. The Angel of Death was never unarmed. *How hadn't I seen them?* Anonasai looked at her reflection in the glass doors. *Smart* – a one-way film covered the glass that acted like a mirror.

'Lay down on the ground with your arms out wide,' ordered the man.

Constantine made his eyes turn white and looked at the man with the megaphone giving the orders. He read the name on the golden badge: Sergeant M. Hitchcock. Sasha was on the ground and looked at Anonasai as she stood. 'Anonasai, get on the ground!' pleaded Sasha.

'I will not be captured here.'

'Don't worry, sister, wherever they take you, you'll be free in no time,' reassured Constantine.

'How can you be sure of that?' asked Sasha.

'In the Makino, nothing can hold us, and nothing can break us,' replied Constantine and Anonasai in unison.

'Sasha Silca! Stand and walk backwards towards my officer's voice,' ordered Sergeant Hitchcock.

Sasha stood and took one last look at Anonasai before walking backwards towards the male voice yelling at her until hands grabbed her and took her to the back of an Aston Martin Firestorm police vehicle.

'You are safe now, ma'am,' assured an officer.

Sasha shook herself free from the officer's hands and read his badge: H. Cupid.

'Hermes,' announced Sasha with relief.

'Yeah, I heard news The Head and Princess were in trouble, so I came to help.'

'Are you here to rescue the Princess or only The Head?'

'Both, I'm her lifeline.'

Sasha raises an eyebrow.

'Yeah, I know, figure of speech.'

'Mick O'Neil, stand and walk backwards to my officer's voice.'

Constantine stood and looked at his sister as she mouthed, 'Love you, brother.' He stood there for a while until he was yelled at to get moving. Constantine mouthed back his love for his sister before walking away. As he walked a tear rolled down his face; in the many centuries they have lived, not once had Anonasai said she loved him. So, he straightened himself up as he walked backwards until an officer grabbed him and took him to the car with Sasha. He turned around to see a familiar face. 'Hermes, great timing as always.'

'You're safe now, sir.'

'Yes, well, the only loose end is my sister.'

Hermes saw three officers running to her location. 'Sir,' said Hermes earnestly.

Constantine looked over to see a commotion as his sister was forced to stand. Police officers and agents argued as to who had more authority over the other. Either way, his sister was right, his plans always had holes in them and this time he'd majorly screwed up.

CHAPTER 28

The South Row Police Department placed evidence on Anonasai, and after a three-month trial, she was taken away to Nightstone Max Prison. There she spent a week in a communal cell with a detoxing drunk who threatened to kill her before being transferred to a padded isolation cell to spend the rest of her fifty-year sentence.

She didn't mind the peace and quiet. It was soothing. The padded cell was like a giant queen-size bed. What she did mind was when her silence was broken for mealtimes and interrogations. Officer Whippet would come every day around three o'clock. At first, the timing meant nothing until she understood the significance of this. So, she played along. Her lawyer was irrelevant, so she fired him, giving up her Miranda rights.

Officer Whippet was stunned by this and called that

session to an end. Anonasai knew what she was doing and walked freely to her padded cell and slept. She didn't eat dinner. Dinner slop was a joke, beef was charred, potatoes sandy and the vegetables were served frozen. The water was drinkable. Hermes came around every day to check in, but she told him to *fuck off*, she didn't need him. This was Nightstone Max – unescapable.

That's when an idea came to her. She grabbed her pillows and placed them in the far-right corner of the room and wrapped a blanket around them. It fell over twice but it still looked like a body. She then stood beside the door that night. When morning dawned, she looked at her handy work.

Breakfast came. She knew who was on duty that morning – a couple of newcomers who still had empathy for inmates. They slid in her breakfast through a slit in the door and left. The bland porridge was drowning in milk with a Pink Lady apple as a side dish. An hour later she could hear their conversation.

'Her tray isn't here,' said a male voice.

'Perhaps she is still eating?' said a younger male voice.

'No, we'll give her an hour, which is what the warden said,' replied the first guard.

'I don't know. Maybe she is sick today,' suggested the young guard, who opened the viewing port to see the inmate in the far-right corner of the room. 'Oh, poor thing, she's curled up in the corner. See I told you she is sick.'

'You did a visual check on a pro-assassin.'

'Don't be so harsh,' gasped the young guard. 'What if she is dead? She didn't eat dinner last night.'

'She never eats dinner,' snapped the first guard. He scanned his key card next to the cell and waited for the low buzz. The door swung inwards nearly crushing Anonasai as it stopped mere inches from her. From the viewing glass she saw the guards in black uniforms with rifles strapped to their sides and with two additional smaller weapons. As they walked to the supposed body, she walked out of the padded cell.

The young guard pulled back the blanket and looked stunned at the two folded pillows. The first guard looked around the cell but it was empty. 'Where is inmate six seven four six?'

'Don't use numbers like that! She has a name.'

'Shut up, where is she?'

They heard the cell door close.

'No, no, no, goddamn it!'

'Anna let us out!' yelled the young guard.

The first guard looked at his young colleague. 'You need breaking-in more, Private. You're too soft.'

Anna smiled as she walked down the smooth stone hallway past many prisoners begging to be set free. Some screamed, yelling louder and louder. Before long, a guard ran down the hall and grabbed her, pushing her into another padded cell. Her twenty seconds of freedom were over thanks to a protective guard, a guard who didn't listen to her, to Hermes who didn't take *fuck off* as an answer. Now she was back in a padded cell with a guard looking down at her.